HUNTED

BY

SHADOWS

SHADOWBORN SERIES BOOK ONE

ERIN O'KANE

Hunted by Shadows

Book One of the Shadowborn Series

By Erin O'Kane

DEDICATIONS

To my husband and wonderful family for believing in me,
I couldn't have done this without you.

ALSO BY THE AUTHOR

Hunted by Shadows

Lost in Shadows: Coming soon

By Erin O'Kane and K.A. Knight:

Circus Save Me

Circus Saves Christmas: Coming soon

The Last Hope: Coming soon

Prologue

"*R*un, little wolf."

Fear pulses through my body at the sound of his voice, my inner wolf screaming to be let out. My heart pounds against my chest, as I look around the dark, dingy room for a way out. Trapped. My dirty, unwashed hair clings to the tears rolling down my seven-year-old cheeks.

I hear footsteps making their way towards me. I would have known it was him by the sound of the heel of his shoes clipping against the floor, even without him announcing his presence with his favourite chant. As the sound of his feet gets louder, so does my breathing. I know all too well the fate that awaits me on the other side of the door.

"*Run, little wolf.*"

My fists clench as I fight the change, my nails digging into my palms as they transform into claws. My skin tingles. I don't need to look to know that fur is sprouting along my body. Closing my eyes, I force my wolf to back down, knowing that turning into my wolf form is exactly what he wants.

Keys clank in the lock and the door squeaks as it's pushed open. Shadows creep into the room, almost seeming to crawl towards me. I force my weak, battered body to stand up, glaring at my tormentor as he fills the doorway.

"*Hello, little wolf.*"

Chapter One

The myriad sounds and smells of the hospital batter my heightened senses as I walk into the emergency department. The fluorescent artificial lighting above me irritates my eyes, and the whining and whirring of the multitude of machines make it difficult to focus on what the portly, sweating man in front of me is trying to tell me as he flags me down. Don't even get me started on the various scents and odours that are overwhelming my enhanced sense of smell. It may be early in the morning, but it's still just as busy here. It's enough to make most shifters turn tail and run, excuse the pun. But not me: I work as a nurse in A&E – or the emergency department, as the Americans call it. I have lived here for six years now and I still can't seem to lose my Briticisms. I love working here. Well, human-Ari does. I can feel wolf-Ari cringing at the assault on our senses. She has been getting more and more agitated recently; it has been too long since we last shifted.

It's dangerous for a shifter to ignore their inner animal for too long. Suppressing these instincts tends to have disastrous consequences, both for the shifter and those who happen to be too close. Thankfully this is rare but, working as a nurse, I have seen my fair share of rogue shifter injuries. Not that humans are privy to this kind of knowledge – they only know them as unfortunate and horrendous muggings. Even now I can feel my wolf eyeing up the man in front of me, my eyes wandering to his neck where I can see his pulse fluttering away like a startled rabbit under his skin. He would be easy prey. Having consumed one too many pies, he would be slow, and he would be no match for my superior strength... I shake my head to get rid of these thoughts and force a smile at him instead, pretending I know what he has been going on about. These humans are so slow to communicate what they want, like they have all the time in the world. All I would need to do is to jump forward and snap his neck and, bang, life over.

Now, now, Ari, stop looking at the nice humans as prey, I scold myself. That would be a spectacular way to lose my job and reveal the existence of shifters to the human world. Not to mention being hauled in by ASP – the Allied Supernatural Protectors, who are our version of the police. They govern us and make sure we keep the peace and, most importantly, don't reveal ourselves to the humans. I have a good setup here; I'm not prepared to blow my cover by going feral.

A sudden quiet catches my attention and brings me back to where I am: at work, behind the nurses' station, staring at the man in front of me. Seeing the expectant look on his face, I know he has asked me a question, and I haven't got a clue as to what it was. *Way to go, Ari,* I scold myself again. I seem to be doing that a lot lately. Thankfully I am saved from answering as an announcement comes from the overhead speaker system:

'Trauma call, adult male trauma. ETA five minutes. Trauma team to resus one please.'

Making my apologies to the startled man waiting for my answer, I hurry over to resus station one, waiting to be briefed.

Anticipation and excitement run through me as we are given our roles for the upcoming trauma patient. This is what I have trained for and what I love doing. Hearing someone call my name, I look up and smile as I see who is walking towards me.

"Good evening, Dr Daniels," I say with a smile to the handsome doctor, and he pulls a face at my choice of greeting.

"You know I hate it when you call me that," he replies, but the smile on his face takes any sting out of his words. Eric Daniels is gorgeous, with his blue eyes, short blond hair and dazzling smile. It's no wonder he is a hit with all the ladies. Gorgeous, kind and a doctor? He even has me eyeing him up when no one is looking. I grin at his comment, and he takes a step towards me, placing his hand on my arm, his face lighting up at the physical contact. The smile drops from my face as I take a small step away, feeling guilty as I see a brief look of hurt flash across his eyes.

So what's the problem, you ask? A gorgeous man, who has a good job and is interested in me – sounds like a win, right? Problem is, he is 100% human, and I can't date a human, even if I'm pretending to be one. We met at one of my crazy housemate's parties, where she had forced the two of us together with a quick "Have you met Ari?" before disappearing into the crowd. She is always trying to set me up, and Eric is just one of the latest men she deemed suitable. Victoria Smith, or Tori as I know her, is my best friend and flatmate. Being a witch, she blends in well with the humans, given the fact that she is one, albeit with a few extra... abilities. Typically shifters don't get on with other supernaturals, preferring to stick with our own kind, but we hit it off straight away. Knowing what I am, she should know better than to keep trying to set me up with humans.

Focusing on the task at hand, I try to centre my attention on the briefing, acutely aware of Eric standing next to me. Maybe Tori is right: perhaps it has been too long since I've gotten laid, and a tumble in the sheets with Dr Gorgeous wouldn't do any harm, right? As if he can sense my thoughts, I feel Eric's attention turn to me. Thankfully the paramedics burst into the trauma room and the controlled chaos begins. A brief fight with my wolf begins, as with all major trauma cases such as this. I am a wolf, after all, and the smell of blood fills the air and makes her restless. She wants out, especially when I haven't shifted for so long.

Pushing my instincts aside, my senses hone in on my patient, my attention fully on him as I focus on my job of keeping him alive. My sensitive hearing can pick up his gurgling wheeze from here; I am positive it's a punctured lung. I continue my assessment of the patient alongside the medics, passing on my judgements to Eric, who agrees without question. He knows that I know my stuff, and I have yet to be wrong about a diagnosis. Nurses often have an intuition about patients, and thankfully that's what my abilities are passed off as. Minutes pass, although it might be hours, as time passes strangely in emergency situations. Finishing my primary survey, I lift the patient's arm to get a better look at his side, although I pause when I see strange bruising, a sense of worry filling me at the unusual site of the injury.

"Dr Daniels, I think he is wounded on his back as well," I inform him, keeping my voice calm despite the sense of urgency I am feeling.

With the help of the team, we are able to lean the patient to one side so we can look at his back. Cursing sounds come from the nurses on my side of the patient, but I pay no attention, my gaze fixed on the mutilated back of the patient. My wolf rushes to the surface, demanding to be let free. *Protect, find, kill, run.* Her demands run though my head, each one louder than the last. My bones ache at the force of her trying to shift, my front teeth elongating into sharp points. My fingers grasp the bed in front of me, the fabric tearing under my grip.

"Ari." Hearing my name jerks my gaze up to the person who is trying to gain my attention: Eric. I take some deep breaths to keep my wolf under control, pretty sure my already unusual eyes are softly glowing with my wolf this close to the surface.

"Go take a break," he orders, his tone of voice not giving me any choice other than to obey. But his eyes are soft, understanding... Shaking my head, I walk away. I don't have time to think about Eric right now. My steps are hurried as I walk to the ladies' changing rooms.

Bracing my arms against the sink, I look up into the mirror above me. My unusual amber eyes are reflected back out at me, made even more unnatural by the supernatural power that is making them glow softly as my wolf walks under my skin. I shudder as she tries to force the change again. My mind returns to the patient and his mess of a back, to the symbol that had been marked, no, fucking *carved* into his back: the very same symbol that I have tattooed on my upper back, just over my spine and in between my shoulder blades. The symbol depicts a wolf howling to the moon, covered in shadow, representing the pack that it belongs to.

I place my shaking hands into the sink and let the cold water wash over them before splashing some of the water onto my face. *Calm the fuck down, Ari; think.* I pace the room. This isn't just a random shifter attack, not with Shadow Pack's symbol carved into a random human's back. Were it any other pack's symbol, I could rule it out as some sort of punishment; shifter justice is brutal. But in the middle of the US, why would a human be carved with the symbol of a pack that is over 3,000 miles away, in the UK? My former pack. There's only one conclusion. I take a deep breath and look at my reflection again as I admit to myself what I have feared since the day I arrived in the US.

They have found me.

Pushing aside the rising feeling of dread, I walk to my locker where I have stashed my personal belongings. I shake my hair out of its hospital-required ponytail, letting the brown and gold strands fall across my face, creating a shield between me and the rest of the world.

Right, that's enough of the pity party, I think to myself, never being one for self-pity. If I'm going to get out of this, I need to be strong, not falling apart in the locker room of the hospital.

Pushing away from the locker, I open it, pulling my mobile phone from my jacket pocket. Seeing a message from Tori, I tap on it, frowning. She doesn't usually text me when I'm at work, unless she wants me to pick up take-out on the way home. A woman after my own heart.

Tori: So that was weird. Some hottie just came to the apartment asking after you. He felt like wolf to me. Had that growly Alpha feel to him. I kept it vague, saying you were out.

Shit. I keep my distance from shifters, and I certainly don't give any of them my address. Tori has this built-in sense where she can get a 'feel' of someone and their supernatural abilities, and so far she has never been wrong. If Tori says there is a wolf asking after me, then I believe her. Running my hand through my hair, I sort through my options. There is protection around our flat, and as long as he isn't invited into the house he shouldn't be able to get in. Picking up my phone again, I send off a text to Tori.

Me: Don't let him in, I'm not expecting anyone. Just stay alert. Any bad feeling from him?

Almost immediately I get a reply, and I smile as I read the message.

Tori: Girl, I wasn't born yesterday. Besides, you would have told me if you were expecting that piece of hotness. No, no bad feelings. I would have blasted him to next Tuesday if he had. I didn't get much of a feeling off him to be honest.

Me: Thanks for having my back, Tori. I'll pick up Chinese, my treat.

Tori: You know the way to my heart ❤

Laughing at her message, I feel some of the tension leave my body. This mysterious visitor can't be from Shadow Pack if he doesn't have any malicious intent. Anyone from the pack would be radiating bad feelings if they came for me, and Tori would have picked up on it and warned me. So who was this mysterious 'hottie' who was asking after me?

Hearing the emergency bell ringing brings me back to reality. Right, I'm still at work. I'm not in immediate danger, and I'm not going to let those bastards from Shadow Pack intimidate me and ruin the life I have worked so hard to build here. Walking back over to the mirror, I pull my hair back into a ponytail, pleased to see that my eyes have returned to normal. I will need to be careful, though; I can almost see my wolf under my skin. Smiling at myself in the mirror, nurse-Ari is back. Shoulders back and head held high, I walk back out into the emergency department. Patients to save, wolf butts to kick. Just another day in my crazy life.

Chapter Two

 $\mathcal{I}$ shoulder my way into the dingy club, making my way through the crowds on the dance floor towards the bar. It's always busy here, even on a weeknight. Thankfully, once I make it through all the sweaty, dancing bodies, there is a stool at the bar that is unoccupied.

With a grateful sigh I sink into it, feeling the tension of the day ease out of my bones. What a night. After the shift I have had, I deserve a drink, but that's not the only reason I am here tonight. I take a moment to look around the bar. It looks like it used to be a nice place, but years of misuse have left it needing some TLC.

The patrons don't exactly help the image. This particular establishment caters only to supernatural beings. The world that we live in is not as simple as the humans like to believe it is. Werewolves, vampires, Fae, witches and Demons? All real, not to mention the hundreds of other creatures that roam the streets. We're not like the movies portray us; the moon doesn't force me to shift and vampires are not all gorgeous, other-worldly beings – they are dead, after all. Werewolves are just one of many types of shifter; we just happen to have the largest population. We don't all live in harmony – there is always a blood feud going on between several of the races – but this bar is one of the neutral territories in the city where everybody is able to mingle freely. There is still a lot of prejudice, though, and you can almost see the divide in the room between the magic users and the other supernaturals.

Now, I know what you're thinking: why would a person who is determined to stay as far away as possible from other shifters be sitting in a supernatural bar? Unfortunately, it is necessary to show my face occasionally, even for a lone wolf like me. The powers that be at ASP expect us to make appearances. If we don't, they start poking their noses where they don't belong. If you want to stay off their radar, you have to act like they expect you to. So for me, that means showing up at the occasional bar, as would be expected for a young unmated shifter, and keeping out of trouble. Plus, places like this are great for finding out information and listening to gossip.

"Wolf girl, not seen you here for a while."

I spin on my bar stool. I know that growling voice, and only one person would dare call me 'Wolf girl'. Trying to hide a smile, I scowl at the towering wall of muscle in front of me.

"Garett, what have I told you about calling me that? Or shall I refer to you as Grizzly again?" I retort to the bear shifter in front of me.

Laughing, I watch as he starts to pour my usual. Like his inner animal, he is huge, his muscles almost bursting out of his uniform white shirt as he moves around behind the bar. My eyes drop to his ass, and, let me tell you, in his tight black jeans it is a sight to behold. Turning around, Garett raises his eyebrow at me as I'm caught in the act, smirking as he places my beer on the counter in front of me.

"Like what you see, sweetness?" Flipping him off, I take a sip of my cold beer, trying to ignore the blush that covers my cheeks.

Laughing, Garett turns to serve a willowy Fae at the other

end of the bar. Man, I really need to get laid. But he is the closest thing I have to a friend in the shifter community, and I am not going to ruin that by jumping his bones. The club is crowded, people pushing for a space at the bar and trying to get served, all except for a clear circle of space around me. I smirk into my beer. This is another reason I came to this particular bar: no one is going to mess with someone who has a grizzly bear looking out for them.

Falling into my own thoughts, I take a sip of my drink, not really paying attention to the people around me until I feel a tingling down the back of my neck. Someone is watching me. I slowly sit up straighter in my chair, trying not to tip them off that I know I'm being watched. My wolf pushes to the surface, wanting to protect me. An uneasy hush falls near me as the supernaturals closest to me feeling my power start to emerge. They might not all be shifters, but they can feel the waves of Alpha strength rolling off me.

All shifters are born with a certain amount of power, and within a pack our ranking is determined by how strong that is. Certain shifters will be powerful enough that they can claim positions within the pack, such as Beta or Gamma, the second and third in command after the Alpha. Some of these shifters will have Alpha power, which means they have the potential to become head of the pack. This is why I stay away from most shifters, as I am unusually strong for a female shifter. I happen to have Alpha power, although I have never wanted to claim that responsibility. This puts a target on my back, either because I am a threat that needs to be taken out, or I am viewed as a prize for the strongest male to win. That doesn't work with me, hence the lone-wolf attitude.

The people nearby start shuffling away from me, aware that something is happening around them, even if they are not sure what that is. Garret stalks towards me, his eyes moving around the bar, looking for the threat that has sent my senses into overdrive. His shoulders look tense and he braces himself against the bar, leaning towards me. His eyes widen a fraction with surprise at my show of power, as he moves his gaze from the crowd to study my face.

"When was the last time you shifted?" he asks. "I know you don't like doing it, but you're putting yourself and everyone around you in danger. Plus, you're putting off my customers." He says the last part with a sly smile to take the sting out of his scolding, although his posture is still tense.

This is a long-standing argument of ours. The tingling has stopped, so whoever it was has moved on, most likely because of the scene I unwittingly caused. I close my eyes, calming myself. *I am in charge, I am in control, I am not in danger.* I open my eyes, seeing Garett's look of concern quickly turn to amusement.

"Want to get naked together?" he asks with a grin, although I'm sure I hear a note of worry in his voice.

I laugh at his comment, rolling my eyes and taking a sip of my drink to hide the blush that's covering my cheeks.

"Oh Garret, how could I say no to such a proposal?"

Garett and I have shifted together on occasion. I may distance myself from other shifters, but at a base level, wolves are pack animals. It feels good to rub my fur against someone else, even if that someone is a massive seven-foot bear. Garett may look ferocious in his animal form, but really he is a fuzzy, over-protective mother hen. He may play it off like he wants to see me naked, but his first instinct is to protect me. Plus, his favourite hobby seems to be making me blush. I place my beer back on the bar, running my finger through the condensation forming on the glass as I muse over today's events.

"Garett. Have you heard of any... unusual attacks on humans recently?" I sense him pause and I glance up to see him frowning, before he continues polishing the glass in his hand.

"What kind of attacks?" he asks, his voice low as he glances around the bar, eyeing the goblin on the stool closest to me. I sigh.

"A human turned up at the hospital today barely alive and had a pack symbol carved into his back," I tell him quietly, aware of how many supernatural ears may be listening.

Garett instantly stiffens, his eyes briefly flashing amber as he fights his bear for control. His eyes flick to my shoulder, as if he can see the tattoo between my shoulder blades. While shifting doesn't require a person to take their clothes off, it is easier to shift naked, so he has seen my tattoo on several occasions.

"Any particular pack symbol?" he asks, his voice deeper and more gravely than it had been a moment earlier.

I nod, verbal confirmation not necessary for the direction of his thoughts. Crushing the glass, sharp shards explode from his hand and cover the bar as his control slips. I raise my eyebrows at him as I see blood dripping from his fist, gesturing for him to let me have a look at the damage he may have caused. Garett doesn't know the specifics of what happened between me and my pack back in England, but his suspicions make him very protective of me. I shake my head as I look at his fist. Had he been human he would need it cleaned and stitched up, but being a shifter he is protected from infection and would be healed within an hour. I pluck out a few pieces of embedded glass, raising my eyebrows at his noises of complaint.

"You grizzlies are so easy to rile up," I tell him with a small smile, letting go of his fist.

The bleeding has already stopped. He looks at me with a serious expression, leaning closer to me.

"If they have found you, you will need protection."

My inner wolf does not like the comment. Hell, I don't like that comment – when we have proven that we can protect ourselves just fine. I have managed on my own for six years, and for 18 before that in the hellhole that my former pack had called 'home'. I'm just about to whoop his ass and give him a piece of my mind when I feel a strong presence behind me.

"I guess it's a good thing I'm here, then," a deep velvety voice remarks. I grudgingly look over my shoulder at the person invading my space. Usually, I would be kicking serious butt if someone snuck up on me like this. However, I know that voice all too well.

"Oh god. What did I do to deserve you being here?" I curse my luck, putting my head in my hands on the bar.

I'm a nurse; I save people's lives on a daily basis – so why do the gods seem to hate me so much? Despite me wishing it otherwise, I can feel his presence coming closer as he takes a seat in the vacant bar stool next to me. My 'piss off' vibes must not be clear enough tonight. Throwing a glare at the imposing werewolf next to me, I look back at Garett, who is watching the both of us with an amused smile. There are only a handful of reasons why Alexander Parker, Beta of the local wolf pack, would be here sitting next to me. Judging from Garett's relaxed posture, he obviously isn't concerned for my welfare; he wouldn't let me get hurt in his bar. Besides, I stay as far away from the Moon River Pack as possible.

"Why is he here? Can't I get any peace in this city?" I complain, before standing up to lean over the bar, taking a bottle of whisky. I am going to need something stronger than beer to get me through tonight. What I haven't anticipated is how far away the bottle is, requiring me to lean far enough that my mid-thigh-length skirt rides further up my leg. I hear a very male appreciative hum behind me, and I immediately straighten, catching said Beta staring at my ass.

"Really?" I raise my arms in an 'are you serious?' gesture.

Alex has the audacity to shrug, a small smile tugging at the side of his mouth, not in the slightest bit ashamed at being caught ogling me. Glancing over at Garett for support, I glare at him as he raises his hands in a 'not my issue' gesture before heading to the other end of the bar. I don't miss the look that he gives Alex before he leaves, though, nor Alex's respectful dip of his head. Shaking my head, I turn my attention back to the bottle in my hands and pour myself a generous glass of whisky. Men are weird.

"Ari," he starts, the hairs on my arm standing on end and my breath catching at his deep voice saying my name as he pulls his bar stool closer to mine.

Traitorous body. I turn and finally give him my full attention. He hasn't changed since I last saw him. The stubble across his lower face frames his jaw, emphasising his model-worthy cheekbones. His face has a raw, unmistakable masculinity to it, making him annoyingly handsome. Enviably long dark eyelashes frame his piercing grey eyes, and his dark hair falls in waves to just above his shoulders. Perfect for gripping on to. *Whoa, calm down, girl.* My eyes flare golden as my wolf walks under my skin, making all of my baser urges come to the surface. Of course, Alex notices this, his eyes glinting with the hunger I am all too familiar with seeing in the eyes of male shifters. Ignoring him, my eyes continue their assessment of his body, passing his broad shoulders and running down his chest. His loose t-shirt can't hide the muscle under there, the fabric straining against his biceps as he leans towards me, his gaze intense. Even sitting, I can tell he is tall, making me feel petite, which is a feat in itself as I stand just under six foot.

"What do you want, Alexander?" I ask, forcing my eyes away from his body, which is taking considerably more effort that I care to admit. Taking a swig of my drink, I savour the burn of the whisky, focusing on the comforting feeling rather than the sizzling power that is radiating from the male next me. He leans closer to me again, placing a hand on the bar, knowing better than to touch me right now. He may make my wolf want to rip his clothes off and have her wicked way with him, but he would be foolish to touch a shifter this close to losing control.

"Come to Moon River Pack," he says, his tone not leaving room for debate, the type of voice that is used to being obeyed.

This is not the first time Moon River Pack has tried to get me to convert, nor the first time Alex has asked – although it has been a while since the Alpha stopped sending eligible bachelors to try to convince me. I thought they finally had the message, but apparently not.

"Let us protect you."

Oh, hell no. I slam my glass back onto the bar, albeit maybe a little harder than necessary, and push to my feet.

"I don't need anyone to protect me. Especially not some male who feels he has some claim over me," I bite out, my voice more guttural than it had been previously.

Tasting blood on my lip, I know that my fangs have descended. My wolf is just as pissed off as I am at the insinuation that we cannot protect ourselves. This is just one of the many reasons why I can't stay in a pack. I am too dominant for most shifters and I am not content to be some trophy mate for those who wish to dominate me.

Striding away from the bar, I am aware of how quiet it is, many having turned to watch the scene unfold. I see Garett glaring daggers at Alex, but he makes no move to defend my honour. I snort. Useless males. I am getting out of here before I tear into someone, literally.

"Ari, wait. We need you."

I come to a stop and a frustrated sigh passes my lips. It's not so much the words that make me stop, but the hint of desperation in his voice. Part of me wants to tell Alex to go fuck himself, but the other part of me wants to hear him out. It would take a lot for an Alpha male such as Alex to come to me for help. However, I really, REALLY don't want to get involved in pack politics. Ever since I arrived in America I have tried to have as little involvement in the local pack as possible. I followed protocol and presented myself to the pack council within 24 hours of arrival in the city. I then politely but firmly told them I did not wish to join the pack, that I wanted lone wolf status. The Alpha knew that forcing me to stay wasn't in anyone's best interest and granted my request. He seemed kind. Alex's older brother had been Beta at the time, though I don't remember his name. What I do remember is that he stood up for me when some of the higher-ranking wolves wanted to stop me from leaving.

I think again about turning Alex down, but a part of me – the damaged, broken part of me – reminds me that I have some atoning to do. That if someone needs help and I can offer it, I have an obligation to do so. With a groan I turn to him, pointing my finger at him accusingly.

"I will give you ten minutes to tell me your problem. After that, I'm out. Oh, and you're buying the next drink,' I order as I stalk towards the bar, ungracefully throwing myself back into my seat, gesturing a smirking Garett over to get our drinks.

Fifteen minutes later I am sitting in a booth, pressed up against six-foot-something of a sexy werewolf, uncomfortably trying to pay attention to what said werewolf is telling me. Alex suggested a quieter spot to discuss 'pack business' and insisted I sit next to him so he could speak quietly. Personally, I think he just likes to be close to me. Our power levels must be similar, as I can feel my wolf pushing for dominance against the waves of Alpha power that are rolling off him. I keep my eyes on the glass of whisky I have been nursing since we sat down. I can't possibly make a rational decision when I am this close to shifting. Fishing my phone from my skirt pocket, I push it across the table.

"Give me your number. I'll think about it and get back to you." There is no room for compromise in my voice, and I think he can sense that; he doesn't push the matter, merely entering his number and nodding to me before leaving the booth.

Once he has gone, I feel like I can breathe again. I may not like the guy, but I have to admit he is one sexy male. I mull over what he revealed to me. His pack is having problems carrying pregnancies to full term, or even conceiving in the first place. Turns out their pack medic was killed in an attack last year. Even I had heard of the attack; a massacre on that scale made ripples in the supernatural community. It even made it to the human news, although they were under the impression that there had been a large fire that had killed sixteen people at the local woodland retreat. After that, the pack had attempted to recruit me again, which I politely but firmly declined.

And now they are trying again, but this time they want me for my nursing skills. It helps that I am a werewolf too; they won't trust anyone who isn't. Not that I know how I can help them. Sure, I have completed my emergency birthing training as all nurses do, but I don't know the slightest thing about pregnancy health – I'm not a midwife! But apparently, I am their best option. I think it has more to do with the fact that I am a strong female with lots of power, as I can't be the only available nurse in the shifter community. What Alex doesn't know is that he has played right into my soft spot: I am a sucker for protecting those weaker than me.

I throw back my glass, savouring the burn of the whisky as it glides down my throat. I send Garett a quick text letting him know I'm going for a run. I stand up and throw a mock salute in his direction gesturing to my phone as I walk out of the bar. I don't want to talk to anyone right now; I just need some space and I know he would make me wait for him so he could go with me. I snort to myself at this thought and step out onto the dark streets. I don't need anyone's protection.

Chapter Three

*E*ven this far away from the city I can still hear the noise from the streets, thanks to my enhanced hearing – although I don't have to walk too far into the trees before the sounds fade. I look around at the silent trees surrounding me as I make my way towards my favourite spot to shift. This land is unowned by any of the various packs, so not many shifters come here, and it's far enough away that humans rarely visit either. I walk for about half a mile before I find the right place. Walking up to a twisted old tree, I kneel down beside it, running my hand over its bark before I find the natural crevice where I store my belongings. I learnt the hard way that clothing often goes missing if you leave it unattended in the middle of the forest. Unhurriedly, I strip from my clothing, as only someone who is confident in their body can. There is no room for squeamishness in shifter packs. I'm no Greek goddess, and I eat far too many doughnuts to have a truly flat stomach, but I have an athletic body from a rigorous training regime, so I know I look good, both naked and fully clothed. Even the scars covering my skin aren't enough to make me ashamed of my body. I stash away my clothing and other belongings and walk a little further into the forest.

Closing my eyes, I search for the source of power that resides inside me and reach for my wolf. I open my arms wide, like I'm about to embrace a close friend, and I coax my wolf to the surface. The shift is not pleasant, pain pulsing through my body as my bones shift. This is the price I pay when I don't shift often enough to satisfy my wolf. I drop to my knees and a cry of pain escapes my lips as I let the shift take over my body completely. The process takes a minute or two, but it feels infinite. I really shouldn't let it get so long between shifts. Finally, the pain recedes and I open my eyes, my heightened sight easily allowing me to see in the dark.

I push up onto all fours, shifting my paws into the dirt, stretching my body from snout to tail. With a feeling of freedom, I race deeper into the forest, the trees becoming a blur as I zip between them. I have a bittersweet relationship with my wolf, but this feeling *almost* makes everything worth it.

I savour the rush of the wind though my fur, feeling invincible as time seems to melt away. After a while I pad to a stop near a small stream, lapping at the water eagerly. As I drink I look at my reflection in the water. The same amber eyes stare back at me, and my browny-gold fur is thick and healthy looking. Like in my human form, I am tall for a female wolf, and my powerful back legs make me fast and strong. I take another drink from the water and I realise that the forest has gone quiet. Sure, it's night-time and I'm a predator, so wildlife tends to disappear, but my hearing can pick up sounds from over a mile away, and I know this silence is unnatural.

My body tenses as I hear a twig snap about ten meters behind me. I discreetly sniff the air to see if I can scent who is stalking me, without tipping them off that I know they are there. Wolf. Alex said Moon River would leave me alone until I responded, so unless they are defying their Beta, this is a wolf from a different pack. The wind shifts, bringing the scents closer to me. Scratch that, more than one wolf. Five, if my senses aren't betraying me. I internally curse myself. I should have picked up on this earlier. If I shifted more often and my skills were not so rusty, they never would have been able to sneak up on me.

Turning to face my stalkers my hackles raise as I sink into a defensive stance. Five male wolves of various sizes face me in a loose semi-circle. I don't recognise any of them, although the one in the middle keeps grabbing my attention. He is a brute, both in size and by the power rolling off him. He has dark grey fur, but his most noticeable feature is the scars that run from his mangled left ear across to his snout. While I believe I'm stronger, he has the advantage of numbers.

I think that I should give them a chance and not assume; they may not be here to attack me. I mean, sure, they snuck up on me in the dark, but they may just want to talk... The large one in the middle snarls and takes a menacing step closer, the other wolves following his lead. Okay, so they aren't here to talk.

A growl passes my mouth as my lips draw back over my teeth, baring my fangs, my fur standing on end as my ears flatten against my head, ready for them to attack as I wait to see what they plan to do. I need to even the numbers if I'm going to stand a chance. At a growl from the grey wolf at the front, the two wolves at the edges break off from the group to circle around behind me.

My wolf is not happy with this at all. A strong wave of power surges through me, almost knocking me off my paws. I can see when the wolves sense it, as they come to a stop. The grey wolf's gaze narrows on me as he growls a command to approach again. The wolves do as commanded, but much more hesitantly. I grab onto the Alpha power running through my bloodstream and push my intent into it, commanding the wolves to stop, bow down to me, stay.

Immediately two of the wolves drop, whining in the process. The two wolves flanking the grey wolf stumble as my command weighs heavily on them. Though they don't possess Alpha power, they are possibly Beta or Gamma in ranking. Grey continues to stalk towards me, my command slowing his steps and makes him more cautious. I may be stronger than him, but he has more practice at this than me.

Shit.

I turn on my heels and bolt as fast as I can from my pursuers. I don't care where I'm going; I just know I need to get away. I can hear more than one set of paws behind me, and glancing over my shoulder I can see Grey and one of his Beta wolves, while in the distance the other Beta is stumbling to his paws, fighting my command. I face the direction I am running in – I need to pay attention and I need a plan. I may be fast for a female, but there is no way I can outrun a full-grown Alpha-level male wolf.

I have more tricks up my metaphorical sleeves, but I won't use them unless there is no other choice. I have been running from my demons for the last six years, and I swore I wouldn't use that power again unless my life depended on it.

Hot, searing pain flares in my right flank as I am bitten. I turn and fiercely bite into the closest thing to me, which turns out to be Grey's shoulder. We tumble to the ground in a tangle of claws and teeth as I slash at his belly. He growls at me, letting go of my flank. I back away from him with a limp, trying to keep the weight off my back leg. I see his shoulder is oozing blood, which fills me with a sickening satisfaction. The other wolf that was chasing me stalks closer, trying to get around behind me.

Growling, I dart forward, slicing my claws across his face. Whilst I am distracted, Grey pounces on me, pinning me to the ground, biting into my shoulder, mirroring the wound I had caused on him. I howl out in pain as he bites me, pain and blood loss making my vision dim. I can feel the other wolves begin to creep closer and I know that I have lost this fight. Knowing I have no other choice, I close my eyes and will that dark little piece of my power to come forward, and I become shadow.

I stumble in my shadow form towards Garett's bar. At some point within my shadow form I have changed back to human, although I'm not sure when. My wounds and the fizzling adrenaline is making me dizzy. I'm not sure why I even came here, or when I decided that Garett was my 'in case of emergency' person, but I know deep in my bones he will help me. I wait in the dark alley by the employee entrance, knowing that he will be leaving soon. It must be about four in the morning, and thankfully it's quiet out, just a few drunks milling around. I collapse against the wall, letting it take my weight. The dripping sound of my blood should concern me, but there are worse things out here to worry about than werewolves and I can't find the energy to care. At the sound of a door opening, I look up. I have never been more glad to see Garett in all my life.

"Garett," I call out, surprised at how weak my voice sounds. He looks up, immediately alert, confusion clouding his features as he looks around the dark alley.

"Ari?" he asks, taking a step in my general direction.

I wonder at his confusion and realise I'm still in my shadow form. He can't see me. I close my eyes again, and with colossal effort I focus on pulling the darkness back inside my body. I let out a small cry of pain, falling to my knees at some point during the process. I know it has worked when the pain hits me at full force and I hear Garett swear, his large form filling my vision.

"Hey Big Bear." I smile up at him as he runs his hand gently through my tangled locks.

He swears again at my affectionate tone, and glances at my very naked body, covered in blood. I hear a menacing growl coming from him, and I glance at his face, seeing his eyes are glowing, indicating that his bear is close to the surface as he looks around the alley for my assailant. I should probably be worried that I am inches from a shifter who is close to losing control, but I know he won't hurt me. I gently place my hand on his chest to gain his attention, and frown when I see blood caking my skin, transferring to his shirt with my sluggish movements.

"Oops, I've stained your shirt. I'll have to get you a new one," I tell him. Or he could just take his shirt off, I wouldn't mind.

I giggle at this thought, then I let my head rest against his chest in exhaustion, the events of the evening catching up with me. I should probably be worried. I *never* giggle, but the giddy feeling of being safe and protected is making me act strange. Or it could be the blood loss.

"Ari, forget the fucking shirt. I need to get you somewhere safe, but this is going to hurt like a bitch. Are you ready?" My bear has a potty mouth tonight. I should get him a swear jar for Christmas.

Fighting another giggle, I nod, reaching up and running my hand through his messy hair. He shifts his arms around me, picking me up, cradling me between his arms. I cry out; I was not prepared for the jarring movement. My vision dims as I feel Garett pick up his pace, trusting that he will take me somewhere safe.

"I've got you Ari, you're safe."

I think I can hear Garett talking to me, saying sweet things that no one has ever said to me before. It's nice. Shame it's probably just a hallucination. As unconsciousness comes to claim me, something keeps repeating in my mind, an uneasiness I can't seem to shake. The satisfaction in the grey wolf's stare chases me into the darkness. It was almost like me shifting into my shadow form was what he wanted all along.

Chapter Four

I wake up to someone stroking my hair. It's a nice, but unfamiliar feeling. I smile and arch my back into the warm body behind me. It's been too long since I shared a bed with anyone. A warm hand presses against my stomach, pulling me closer and I find that someone is *very* happy to see me this morning. I rack my brain to try and recall the events that led to this situation. How have I ended up in bed, naked, with a stranger? At least, I hope it's a stranger. Oh please, god, let me not have slept with my ex. Or worse, Dr Eric Daniels. If I sleep with him, I want to be able to remember it.

I attempt to move my body, preparing myself for the worst. I go to look at the male pressed to my back, when I feel a hand move on my leg – on my other leg, from an angle that does not match to the body behind me. Unless I've slept with Mr Fantastic, which I doubt, there is more than one person in the bed with me.

Jolting up from the bed I hear some very disgruntled male voices as I break free. I stumble to one knee, cursing in pain as my legs give way. Spinning around, I look across the bed to see four confused and blinking males – all of whom are totally naked.

"What the fuck?" I practically screech, before realising that I am just as naked.

I reach across and snatch the bed sheets away from them, covering myself up but exposing the men on the bed in the process.

"Will someone please tell me what the fuck is going on? And put some clothes on!" I order. It's seriously distracting with all their naked glory on display.

"I told you she would be pissed off." Relief fills me as I hear Garett's comforting voice and I attempt to push myself to my feet.

I don't know why, but right now I need his arms around me. I can't explain these emotions rushing through me. As if he could read my mind he comes to me, wrapping his arms tightly around me. Which I'm thankful for, because my legs aren't cooperating right now. I bury my face in Garett's chest as I struggle to remember the events of last night. I hear some shuffling around from the comfort of Garett's arms as the men move from the bed to put some clothes on – at least, that's what I hope they are doing. Usually I would be guarding my back – that's rule one, after all – but I know that Garett will handle that for the moment and won't let anything happen to me.

"Will you please explain what is going on? And why the fuck did you bring me here?" I ask, pulling away from his chest, pissed off once again.

I hate being in situations where I don't know what's going on. It makes me cranky. Besides, I just woke up in a bed full of naked men and I have no idea who they are, so I have the right to be a bit pissy. From the scents surrounding me, I know that Garett has brought me to the Moon River Pack. I've not been in this room before, but it smells like them. Wolf packs have a distinct smell, almost like a bond that links them together. Each individual has their own scent, but it gets overlaid with their pack bond. Besides, this is the closest wolf pack for miles.

Why he decided that this was the safest place for me, I don't know. I try to stand again, but the ache in my legs slows me down, causing me to hiss in pain as I stumble back to the bed, still trying to keep my dignity by clutching the bed sheet. All but one of the men has moved from the bed, the last languishing with a smile in my direction, stretched out on the bed like a cat. He crawls closer and rubs up against me, the stubble of his jaw rubbing over my skin as he nuzzles the crook of my neck. If he had been in wolf form, he would have been scent marking me. My eyebrows rise in shock and I shoot a questioning look at Garett, just as the man tries to crawl into my lap. I forgot how touchy-feely shifters are.

"Okay, I'm out." I state dryly as I push to my feet shakily, looking in vain for my clothing.

I don't do well with physical contact, especially from people I don't know. I'm dimly aware of Garett's rumbling growl as he stalks closer to place his hand on my arm, halting my search.

"My god," I say. "You shifters are so touchy." I shake him off just as a figure enters the doorway. "Oh good, another person to make this shitty morning even worse!"

"Everybody out, give us some privacy. Sebastian, please show some restraint. And find Ariana some clothing." I look at Alex's intimidating frame in the doorway and I'm not surprised that they are doing as ordered.

The male from the bed, who I'm assuming is Sebastian, gets up to leave but not before sending a wink in my direction. Pouting at Alex, he exits the room. Garett crosses his arms and stays put, thank goodness. Now it's just the three of us and I feel like I can breathe again. I shoot both of the men a dirty look, before leaning against the nearest wall as I wait for answers.

"Ari, sit down, you're not fully healed yet." Giving Garett the stink eye, I do as he suggested, sitting primly at the end of the bed, very aware that I am fully naked under the sheet that is tightly clasped around me.

I may not be ashamed of my body, but I have scars that tend to invite questions I would rather avoid today.

"Come on, Ari, don't act like I betrayed you. Where else could I take you?" he asks imploringly, sinking to his knees in front of me. "I was going to take you to the bear commune, but you were shifting in and out of shadow. I didn't think you would want them to see that. And I was terrified! Why didn't you tell me you were Shadowborn?" He asks this quietly, but I stiffen at his words.

Shadowborn are rare, even within the supernatural community. With the ability to turn to shadow, they are notoriously trained and used as assassins. In their shadow form no one is safe from them. Being impervious to injury while in this form makes them difficult to kill, which puts a target on their back. Only a handful are born every century or so, and they tend to be killed off early in life, before they learn to master their skills.

The Shadow Pack was named for their higher percentage of Shadowborn, but I was the only one in the last hundred years. What might seem like an honour has only resulted in pain and suffering my entire life. Born into a pack that believes that females are only good for breeding and have no place of power within the pack, my childhood was especially rough. Trained to be strong in body but weak in mind, they didn't anticipate the strength of my Alpha power. Biding my time, I had to wait until I was eighteen until I could make my escape.

Shuddering away from my dark memories, I focus on Garett still kneeling in front of me, and I feel uncomfortable at the look of concern on his face. We are friends; sure, we have flirted on and off for years, but just in a friendly way. While we talk, we have never broached the issues around my old pack or what brought me here, but he knows it wasn't pleasant. Tori knows what I am. Not because I told her, but because her powers revealed to her I was something 'other' and she guessed. I was so shocked when she flat-out asked me that I couldn't hide the surprise on my face. Most Shadowborn learn not to advertise what they are if they value their life.

"I'm fine," I mutter, as I survey my legs. They were shredded last time I saw them, and my shoulder felt like it had been used as a chew toy. Now they ached, but only in a muted way, like a shadow of the pain I should be feeling. Tight shiny pink scars criss-cross my legs, the stage of healing much further advanced that I had expected. Shifter healing is more highly evolved than that of our human counterparts, but with the extent of my injuries my wounds should not be at this stage already. I glance, my expression of surprise clear to see and I raise a questioning eyebrow to Alexander, who is silently watching us with his arms crossed.

"We healed you. You were loosing too much blood; we nearly had to amputate the leg. Which we would have done, too, but your bear here wouldn't let us." Garett half-heartedly growls at this comment, and I have never been more thankful of his friendship.

Forgetting that I am supposed to be pissed off with him, I lean forward and bury my face into the crook of his neck.

"Thank you," I whisper quietly, before pulling away in confusion, only just registering what Alexander had said. "Healed me? You have a witch? I thought you needed a nurse?" I ask, puzzled.

That's why they wanted me here, after all. Only beings that possess magic, such as witches and sorcerers, can 'heal' people. Over one hundred years ago it would be uncommon for there *not* to be a witch in a pack, but it was almost unheard of nowadays. Prejudices run strongly in the supernatural community just as much as in the human world.

I watch as Alexander shakes his head, his shoulder-length hair catching my attention. I have always liked guys with longer hair, more to grab onto. *Down, girl.*

"No, we don't have a witch." He says this with scorn and I raise my eyebrows at his tone, wondering what he would have to say if he found out that I live with a witch. I'm sure it would piss him off and I store this bit of information away for later.

"Do you know nothing of being in a wolf pack? I thought you were raised in a pack. Surely being a lone wolf for a few years hasn't made you forget everything about your kind."

My back stiffens at his comment and I glare at him. How dare he comment on my upbringing like I'm a disgrace to shifter kind! A cold fury fills me, my wolf urging me to bare my fangs and make him sorry for taking such a tone with me. Instead I go still, and even Garett has the good sense to look worried. He knows I am sensitive about my past, and that I never, ever, talk about it. I answer Alexander with a tone that could cut ice.

"I was raised in isolation. Sorry that I don't meet your expectations."

He nods to himself, almost in confirmation, his expression deadly calm. "Is that where your scars came from?"

I give him an 'are you serious?' look, but I keep quiet. I can't believe the audacity of this guy. First he insults my upbringing, then he has the cheek to ask sensitive questions that he has no right asking. I decide not to answer him, he doesn't deserve the answer; he hasn't earned my trust to know about my personal life. Garett, however, has no problem in talking to the asshole leaning against the doorframe. Rising slowly from his crouched position in front of me, he walks menacingly towards Alexander.

"Don't talk to her like that." He says it calmly, like he would when he was addressing one of his difficult customers mouthing off in the bar, but I can see the tension across his broad shoulders.

Pissing Garett off is likely going to end up in someone having broken bones, none of which would be Garett's. I've seen it in the bar before; like the calm before the storm, he will be quiet and reasonable, until you push his buttons a little too far. He has always been protective of me, and I'm still not used to it. It can be suffocating. I've done a pretty decent job of taking care of myself thus far. I glance down at my newly scarred legs again and pause. Perhaps a little help every now and then isn't so bad, right?

Alexander pushes away from the doorframe, giving zero fucks that an almost seven-foot shifter is bearing down on him, excuse the pun. I can feel the Alpha power rolling off him, and I have no idea why Alexander is Beta of this pack and not Alpha, because this guy is *strong* – possibly even stronger than me, not that he will ever know that thought crossed my mind. Coming chest to chest with Garett, they square off against each other and I feel I should step in. With a weary sigh, I stand and walk over to the two infuriating shifters, which is harder than it sounds when you have a limp and are clutching a bed sheet.

With careful movements I take the end of the sheet, securing it under my armpit and hoping it will stay put as I stretch my arms to push on their chests, trying to separate them. Of course, there is no way a female shifter is going to be able to push two fully-grown male shifters. Neither of them pay attention to me, the bastards.

"All right boys, handbags away," I tease, trying to lighten the mood.

At this exact moment, the sheet that has been tasked with protecting my modesty betrays me, dropping to the floor and exposing every naked inch of me. Internally, I curse. Externally, I let a blank expression cross my face and try to keep my body relaxed, as if I haven't a care in the world. Shifters are used to nudity within their packs, so this shouldn't bother me. Of course, *now* I have the men's attention, both of whom have taken a step away from each other.

Men! I raise my eyebrow at them and place my hands on my hips. Alexander is in the process of running his eyes up and down my body, an approving smirk on his face. Garett has the decency to look embarrassed and takes his leather jacket off and hands it to me. I place it over one shoulder, but I refuse to hurry into it because Alexander is attempting to make me feel uncomfortable with his obvious perusal of my curves.

"Like what you see?" I retort, before stalking back to the bed.

I may have added a bit more sway to my walk than usual, so sue me. I shrug Garett's leather jacket on, and it falls to my mid-thigh. I pull it closer around me, enjoying the feel of the leather on my bare skin. Garett's scent surrounds me, a woodsy outdoors smell that makes me feel safe. I decide to keep the jacket for myself; he is going to have to fight me for it back. With a small smile I plonk myself ungracefully back on the bed, crossing one ankle over the other. Now that the situation has been defused – thanks, nudity – I look to Alexander for an explanation.

"Shifters heal better when they have physical contact with other shifters, and it works best with skin-to-skin contact. You needed to heal quickly if you wanted to escape permanent injury. It required four of our wolves to heal your injuries."

My eyes widen as I realise I must have been more seriously injured than I thought. That explains the puppy pile that I woke up in the middle of.

"Why were they all male? I am not prepared to work for a pack where women are not considered as equal," I insist.

I may have come from a pack that was frowned upon for its harsh methods, but I know it's not the only one that considers women as unequal or only there to boost the Alpha male's powerbase.

Alexander shakes his head, a smile on his lips as he does so. "Nothing of the sort. Our Gamma is a female, and the Alpha's wife, and she has just as much authority as he does. They are a true Mated pair, so their power levels are equal."

I raise my eyebrows at this.

Mated pairs are uncommon, and the chance of finding the one being you are destined to be with is rare. You don't see it often, especially when about 50 years back the rate of these pairings dropped even further. Some theorised that because our numbers had dwindled so much through hunters, the chances of meeting our true Mate had dropped even further. It is said that once you accept the Mate bond, you are equal in power and can access the other's strengths.

Alexander clears his throat, bringing me back to the conversation at hand.

"No one was forced to help heal you. We asked for volunteers, and there were quite a few who offered. Although, I think the prospect of spending the night with a beautiful naked woman helped." He ends this last part with a smile that makes me feel a bit flustered.

I lean back on the bed, the leather jacket rising up my thigh, and I can feel the eyes of both men in the room on me. It's quite a sensual feeling, the worn leather brushing my naked skin, acting as the only barrier between the heated gaze of two very good-looking men watching my every move.

"So, what happens next?" I ask, startling both guys.

Alexander gets a contemplative look on his face, and I know exactly where his thoughts have gone.

"Mind out of the gutter, Alexander," I scold, but I say it lightly so as to take the sting out of my words.

This pack has helped me, Hell, they might have even saved my life, whether I like it or not. So, I owe them. Owing a wolf pack and not paying up never ends well for the debtor, whether that debt is money or a favour. I'm not well off – I work as a nurse, for heaven's sake – but I have some savings I managed to 'acquire' when I left my old pack, so if it is money they want I might be able to cough some up. It is the favours I am more worried about. Although, with Garett here, I doubt that he will allow them to demand anything too serious.

"Call me Alex," he says. "I hate being called Alexander. Besides, before I explain anything, the Alpha wants to see you."

Those six words send shivers down my spine, and not the good type of shivers. These are caused by fear. *The Alpha wants to see you.* My breathing picks up as memories engulf me.

Darkness surrounds me. Some people are afraid of darkness, but when it's all you know it becomes comforting. Harsh artificial light fills the room, causing me to hiss with pain and cover my eyes with my dirty hands.

"The Alpha wants to see you."

I dread these words; nothing good ever happens when he wants to see me. I stumble to my feet, my legs shaking from lack of use. I try to exercise in this dark cell they call a room, but if I make too much noise they come check up on me, which I try to avoid. They don't train me anymore, not since I tried to escape. No point training someone who won't do as they're ordered.

I take a few steps forwards, squinting against the light, and glance at my pale hand. I'm so thin that my bones are protruding from my skin, and you can tell I haven't been out in the sunshine for too long. My nails are dirty and chipped. He won't be pleased. He likes the women of the pack to look presentable and neat. Seen but not heard.

The guy who was sent to get me shoves me and I stumble into the wall. I think he just meant to push me along, but the lack of food and sunlight for so long has made me weak. I glare at him and he has the decency to look nervous. I see my reputation still precedes me. Straightening up as much as I can, I step out into the hallway to meet the Alpha.

Tearing myself from the memories, I become aware of someone calling my name. My eyes refocus and I find myself staring into Garett's caring eyes, grounding me to the here and now. I realise at this point he must have been the one calling my name.

"Ari, you're safe here. The Alpha wont hurt you." Alex's voice reaches me and I look over Garett's shoulder to see he has moved away from the wall, and is standing behind Garett.

He turns to look at Garett, his voice turning harsh and revealing his anger. "What the hell happened to her in her previous pack that going to see the Alpha would make her react like this?"

"She will be okay in a minute. Look at her eyes: she is back now. When she is ready to talk, she will," Garett replies. His eyes hold sadness as he watches me, but right now I can't comprehend any meaning behind it.

I pull away from Garett and groan. When I arrived in the US and my flashbacks first started, Tori forced me to see one of the supernatural doctors in the city. They say I have Post-traumatic Stress Disorder, PTSD, where something will trigger me and send me back in my memories. Thankfully it doesn't happen often, but I always feel like crap afterwards. I don't have time to deal with my many issues right now. I need to pull up my big-girl panties and go face the Alpha.

"Right, someone get me some clothes. Let's go see the big guy."

Chapter Five

I glance around the compound as they lead me to see Alpha Mortlock. The compound holds the guise of a woodland retreat, with the main offices being based here. I know what you're thinking: a big macho werewolf pack, running a woodland retreat? Well, they have to earn money somehow. It works well for them. It's far away from human society, they have private space where they can shift without fear of being seen and they rake in the money. This compound is mainly where they run their other businesses from, but they do have a couple of wooden cabins for supernatural guests. Their other compounds are branded as luxury and open to the humans at an exorbitant fee.

The atmosphere seems relaxed, and the people I have passed so far seem happy and well looked after. Everyone we have come across has nodded respectfully to Alexander, or Alex, as he wants to be known, and only sent questioning glances towards Garett and I, not a glare in sight. I imagine that it's not every day that a new wolf and a bear shifter wander through their private compound. Alex wanted Garett to stay behind, which resulted in another argument. Sebastian, the overly friendly naked guy from before, arrived at this point with some clothes for me, which were almost a perfect fit, showing he has a good eye. The argument ended pretty quickly once I stood up and dropped the jacket to the floor to get changed. Sebastian made a comment about helping me into my clothes, which had Garett growling at him. My grizzly bear is grouchy today.

I glance behind me at Garett, and catch him looking at my ass. I snag his gaze and wink at him. My ass does look great in these jeans, and the tight black strappy top reveals just enough to show my assets nicely. My wink has the desired effect as he smiles at my cheeky gesture, but I can still see the tension in the way he holds himself. He seems to have calmed down a lot, although he must be feeling out of his depth in the middle of all these wolves. I turn to face ahead and see Sebastian walking in front of us. Seems he is also going to see the Alpha.

"Hey, Sebastian?" I call. He turns his head and smiles widely at me. "Can I call you Seb?" I ask. He is way too touchy-feely, but I like him, and I feel like I'm going to need a friend here.

"Darling, you can call me anything you like," he replies with a wink.

I chuckle, trying to rid myself of this uneasy feeling as we get closer to the main building. I smile as I feel the sunshine on my skin and take a deep breath of fresh air. As we approach the main building I think back to when I first came here.

I stare at the large compound in front of me. The expensive

wrought iron gates guarding the land are intimidating, but give the impression of an expensive retreat – which, in a sense, I guess it is. Feelings of anxiety attempt to overwhelm me. I try to push these down as I press the button on the intercom built into the wall, requesting an audience with the Alpha. The gates squeak as they open, setting my already fried nerves on edge. The wheels of my suitcase clack on the road as I walk towards the main house, and glance around, taking in any and all escape routes. They are based in the middle of the forest, log cabins are dotted around and a couple of larger buildings surround the main house. My inner wolf is close to the surface. She hated the plane ride and the feeling of being trapped thousands of feet up in the air. I need to let her out, but pack protocol states we present ourselves before we change. Any shift by an unregistered wolf is regarded as an insult or a threat, both of which are dealt with swiftly and brutally.

I am nervous. I have finally escaped the cruel and dictatorial thumb of my pack, and without so much of a 'Welcome to the US' I have to present myself to the local pack, like some sort of prize. I bristle at the thought. I have fought my entire life for freedom, but even in America I am trapped within shifter rules. The pack will want to keep me – I know they will – but I'm not prepared to let that happen. I know how they will see me. A young, skinny, unmated female with a whole load of Alpha power, covered head to toe in bruises and scars. Even if they were cold-hearted bastards and ignored their instinct to protect, they would see the benefit of having that much power around. I feel my limbs begin to shake, and I tell myself it's from exhaustion, not fear. If they were human they might see my small frame, thin from years of malnutrition, and believe this. I can lie to myself all day, but shifters will be able to smell my fear.

I stop a few metres from the main building, and I decide in that moment that I will not let fear control me any longer. I will no longer let others dictate my life. I will no longer be a victim.

Closing my eyes, I push away all of my insecurities and fears. My wolf agrees with me and I feel a surge of strength come from her. We are strong. We can protect ourselves. This is the closest thing to harmony that I have ever felt with my wolf. Opening my eyes, I grab the handle of my suitcase and step through the front door to face the Alpha.

Alpha Mortlock looks just the same as he did six years ago when I first met him. He is handsome, with short sandy-blond hair, and looks to be in his late 30s – but I am pretty sure he is near 70. We can thank our shifter genes for our longer lifespan, which extends to around 140, and we will stay looking youthful for most of our lives.

We were supposed to be meeting in his office, but Alexander had some quick words with Seb as I was getting changed, and the next thing I know, we are meeting in the living room in the main house. I have a sneaky suspicion that Alexander is trying to make the Alpha seem more approachable after my little episode down memory lane. It's thoughtful, but unnecessary.

Mortlock and a beautiful woman, who I'm assuming is his wife, are waiting for us in the communal room. They rise from the soft-looking leather sofas, and Alpha Mortlock takes a step towards me, holding his hand out slowly for me to shake. I turn to glance at Alex, raising my eyebrows in question. What on earth has he said to these people? They are treating me like I'm about to bolt from the building. I straighten my shoulders before turning back to the Alpha and shake his hand firmly. I am no shrinking violet. I am also not the frail, malnourished 18-year-old that I was the last time he saw me.

"Ariana, good to see you again, although I wish it was in better circumstances. Welcome back to Moon River Pack. This is my mate and wife, Lena." He gestures to the woman just behind him, who is beaming at me. "You've met my Beta, Alexander, and this is my Gamma, Isa."

A tall, broad woman peels away from the wall she was leaning against. Her muscles almost put Garett's to shame. Note to self: don't piss her off. Although, with a name that literally means 'strong-willed', I wouldn't expect anything less. Walking towards me, she reaches for my hand, gripping it tight in a death-grip of a handshake. I will my face not to show pain and meet her steely gaze, and I mirror her tight grasp. She smiles slightly at this small display of dominance and slaps me on the back hard enough that I take a small step forward.

'I like her. She can stay," the mountain of a woman states in a thick German accent.

I hear a small whistle of disbelief and glance over my shoulder to see who is making the noise. Seb is watching the exchange with his mouth open in shock.

"I have never seen Isa smile. Ever. What did you do? Did you break her?" he mock-whispers.

The smile drops from Isa's face as she glares at him, promptly causing Seb to mime zipping his lips as he takes a step back into the corner. He may act like everything is a joke, but I don't miss the slight paling of his skin. I smile to myself. I can see why she is the Gamma of this pack, and I am pleased to see such a strong-willed female in a position of power. The structure within a wolf pack will always have an Alpha and a Beta, who is the second in command and acts as a protector of the pack. The role of the Gamma isn't always adopted within packs, depending on the Alpha. Some believe keeping too many powerful wolves around is risky. Their primary role is as enforcer within the pack. Moon River Pack didn't use to have a Gamma. I guess this role was introduced after Alex's brother, the previous Beta, was killed.

"Alpha Mortlock, Lena – pleased to meet you," I say formally, with a bow of my head, my British sensibilities kicking in.

I may not have been there in six years, but I haven't forgotten the manners that we pride ourselves on. I also don't want to piss anyone off within the first ten minutes of being here, so I need to be on my best behaviour. Lena, however, doesn't feel restrained by these formalities and jumps forwards, embracing me in a tight hug. God, these shifters are so affectionate! I'm pretty sure no one notices me flinch as she throws herself on me. I awkwardly pat Lena's back as she hugs me. I'm not really a hugger.

Even Tori and Garett know not to touch me without making their intentions obvious. There have been many occasions where I have nearly thrown someone across the room for simply touching my arm. What can I say? They shouldn't sneak up on me!

Right, that's enough physical touch from strangers for one day. I pull away from the woman latching onto me, although trying to remove her arms is like trying to pull off a squid. I glance around the room for help and see Alexander frowning at me. Guess I wasn't as stealthy at hiding my flinch as I thought.

"Please, no formalities. Welcome to the pack! I'm just so

pleased that we have another strong female joining our ranks! Maybe we can finally get Alex paired off!" she tells me excitedly.

I am still awkwardly trying to remove myself from her grip, sending pleading looks for help towards Seb, and the traitorous little wolf just sniggers at me, enjoying my discomfort. I freeze as her words fully register. *Welcome to the pack.* What the actual fuck?

"I'm sorry?" I ask, my voice coloured with disbelief.

I must not have heard her properly. I did not sign up to join another pack. No. Nadda. Hell NO. I am not prepared to sign my freedom away, and I will not be tricked into joining a pack. I start looking around the room for a way out. I will need to avoid Isa; I won't get past her. I look to the other side of the room where Alexander is standing against the wall by the window. If I'm quick I can get past him and jump through. I shift my stance and the tension in the room rises. Isa and Alexander's positions change to match mine, their limbs poised and ready to attack. Lena realises she has committed some faux pas and takes a step back, glancing to Alpha Mortlock uncertainly.

"Ariana, before you flee from the room and make my Beta chase after you, let's chat. It seems there has been a misunderstanding." Alpha Mortlock's calm voice evaporates the tension in the room, and everyone resumes their previous positions.

Except me, of course. I look at him, my distrust clearly written on my face. I look over my shoulder to Garett. He shrugs at me, leaving the decision up to me. He wouldn't have brought me to these people unless he trusted them to some degree. I nod sharply, deciding I will hear them out. Mortlock takes a seat, and gestures for me to do the same. Lena sits next to him, still looking upset that she has offended me. I'm surprised that she is so... nice. Nice people don't tend to last long in positions of power within the shifter world. I perch on the edge of the seat, ready to spring to my feet at a moment's notice.

"Ariana, we would like you to join our pack. Alex has already told you that we need you here to help us. But we would like to extend the offer indefinitely." I am already shaking my head before he has finished his sentence. Alpha Mortlock tilts his head in question. "Is joining our pack so bad? Do you really want to stay a lone wolf? Never to settle down and feel safe among your own people?"

I sigh. Of course I don't want to be a lone wolf. Shifters as a people belong in a pack; it's part of our nature. All I have ever wanted is to feel safe, welcomed and maybe even loved if that is possible in this cruel fucking world. What he doesn't realise is that I have only ever experienced the worst of my people. My darkest moments have always been at the hands of my pack, my so-called 'family'. Besides, I am fine on my own. I don't need anybody else. I have Tori to watch my back, and I watch hers. That's what friends do: we take care of each other.

Shit. Tori.

Fuck. I am a terrible friend. She is probably going nuts that I didn't come home last night. You do not want to piss off a witch, especially not one as powerful as Tori. I'm lucky that she hasn't tracked me down with a location spell and dragged my ass back to the apartment to explain. I need to get hold of my phone and call her before she blows a gasket.

I also need to make a decision. Alpha Mortlock is watching me expectantly, and Lena has a hopeful look on her face. To turn down a pack, especially when you owe them your life, is a bad idea.

"When you have been through what I have, it makes it difficult to trust others. My pack caused me nothing but pain. I don't mean to be disrespectful, but I cannot join your pack," I tell him. I even let some warmth back into my voice so he knows I am sincere.

"But you were attacked, and you won't be safe on your own. They will probably keep trying. We can offer you protection."

Damn, he does have a point. I may even have to admit to myself that I need help this time. Not that I will ever admit to such a thing out loud.

"I won't join the pack, but I will help in any way I can. I can come back each day for three months, which should give you time to find another nurse. I'll have plenty of protection that way, while I'm working here and on my own. My apartment is warded, so I will be safe at home and I can protect myself otherwise."

The hospital is not going to be pleased with me. I can only offer to stay for three months because I can't afford to take any more time off. I am lucky that today is my day off anyway. As if he could read my mind, Alex pipes up from his corner of the room.

"Of course, we will sort things out with the hospital and reimburse you for your loss of earnings."

Mortlock nods in agreement, running his hand through his neatly trimmed beard. "You are also invited to stay here while you are working for us. We have accommodation attached to the medical room. We will need a nurse around the clock."

I shake my head. I said I would help, not give up my independence. With a sigh, the Alpha nods his head wearily and stands up, looking at those around the room.

"What is said now within this room is to remain a secret," he commands, his Alpha power strong in his words, so strong that I'm not even sure if I could resist his order. Alpha power works a little like persuasion. If you are strong enough, you can fight against it.

He looks back to me, and I am back on alert at the look on his face. "You are Shadowborn," he says. "We will keep your secret but, in return, you must let us train you, both in human form and wolf form. I will not have an untrained Shadowborn on the streets."

Hmm, so someone has told him I am Shadowborn. Or he was there when Garett brought me in and saw me shifting in and out. The last part of his comment sounds a little like a threat and my hackles rise, but I don't disagree with him. I would rather train elsewhere, but I am a liability at the moment. Once I have used my Shadow abilities, it's always harder for me to control it for a while after. Bollocks. I realise too late that I am being backed into a corner. I grumble and look over at Garett, who I see has a resigned look on his face.

"I hate to admit it, Ari, but I don't think you have much of a choice," he tells me, and I remember back to the conversation we had earlier.

I don't want this pack knowing about my abilities. The fewer people who know, the better. Besides, my shadow powers are unstable at the moment. I sigh again. I seem to be doing that a lot.

"Agreed," I tell Mortlock, leaning across to shake his outstretched hand, although I can't help but feel that I have signed my freedom away.

Chapter Six

"*H*e said what?" I ask, dumbfounded, as I stare at the bundle of pink fabric in Seb's arms. I gingerly pluck at the offending item as if it's diseased to see if it really is what I think it is. Yup. It's a fucking dress. A pink, frilly afternoon-tea type dress. I throw the ridiculous garment onto the bed in disgust. I've found that I slip back into calling Alex by his full name when he's pissed me off. Now is exactly one of those times.

"You can tell Alexander to shove this right up his–"

"Is wearing a dress really that big of a deal? I don't get the problem," Garett, the traitor, points out.

I spin around and glare at him hard enough to let him know he is in the dog house. Sorry, the bear house. Wait, bear cave? Oh, whatever. I'm pissed off at him.

"Ooh, Ariana, can I see you in your sexy nurse's uniform?" Seb asks with a smirk as he stalks towards me, a predatory look in his eyes.

"No, you can't. I'm mad at you too. And stop calling me Ariana, it's Ari," I order, my frustration coming through as some of my Alpha power slips into my comment. I see Seb stop in his tracks, his eyes widening slightly as his knees buckle under the force of my order.

"Shit. Seb, I'm really sorry." I am a terrible friend, if that is even what we are. I need to get my shit together.

I didn't realise how low down in the pecking order he is. He is so confident that I assumed he was reasonably dominant. Not strong enough to have a position of power, but not one of the weaker wolves. He certainly doesn't look physically weak. He stands just slightly taller than me, with messy blond hair, and looks like he could star in a movie. I'm talking Zac Efron looks, ladies. Yes, even werewolves go to the cinema. He also looks like he spends a fair amount of time working out; his t-shirt, straining against his muscled shoulders, proves this. I guess looks can be deceiving. Even his vanilla scent is mouth-watering.

His head is bowed, breathing quickened, and I kneel next to him, feeling like the worst person in the world as I place a hand on his shoulder.

"Seb, I am so sorry..." I begin to apologise again when he lifts his head to look at me. His pupils have dilated and a look of pure arousal shines brightly in his eyes. I raise my eyebrows.

"You kinky little shit. That turned you on?" I ask, rocking back on my heels, torn between feeling uncomfortable and amused. I settle on amusement and stand up with a slight laugh.

"I thought I had upset you!" I accuse, still smiling as he stands up from his crouched position. "I'm still not wearing that dress, though," I say, trying to change the subject.

I look over at Garett, and he does not look amused at the whole exchange. In fact, he is scowling at Seb. Such a grumpy bear. Rolling my eyes, I walk over to him, leaning against the wall.

"Has anyone found my phone yet?" I ask. I really need to call Tori. I'm worried that she is going to bring down hell on the pack (quite literally) if I don't speak to her soon.

"I think Alex was looking into it. They are trying to locate where you left your clothes in the woods but they were shredded by the wolves that attacked you..." Garett pauses meaningfully, before looking back at the dress on the bed. "... which is why I don't understand why you won't wear the dress."

I scowl, my temper beginning to rise once again. "I am not wearing that bloody dress! I will go to the social naked if I have to. I don't care what they say. The Queen of England could order it, and I would happily commit treason to get out of wearing that thing," I rant.

Okay, so maybe I am going a little far, but I am not going to be paraded around this pack at the social this evening dressed up looking like a meek little wolf in a pretty pink dress, like I'm some prize to be won. I am already regretting the deal I made with Alpha Mortlock. What I didn't realise is that I am now expected to attend the pack socials, the first of which is this evening, when I will be formally introduced to the pack. Lovely.

Garett shifts in his position against the wall next to me, and I can see from the corner of my eye that he wants to comfort me, but knowing my aversion to touch he changes his mind. He must have decided against arguing any further about the dress, knowing I'm not going to back down on this one. Good decision, buddy.

"I like seeing you in that jacket," he tells me, changing the subject, his voice lower than usual. I look down at the jacket in question. It's the one he gave me earlier, and it makes me feel safe so I have decided to keep it, whether he likes it or not. I'm starting to feel uncomfortable again, all these startling admissions this afternoon putting me on edge. I don't know how to respond to this and I start to pull away, my walls stacking up brick by brick. He must have sensed this, as he stiffens next to me.

Thankfully I am saved from answering as Alex walks through the door, with my phone in his hand, plus what looks like a ladies shirt and a smart pair of jeans.

"God, never thought I would be saying this, but I'm glad to see you," I blurt out. I don't seem to have a filter today, but what I said is true. Not only does he have my phone, but he has also saved me from responding to Garett. Hopefully I can cover up my slip of the tongue by grabbing my phone from his hands, although a glance over my shoulder at Garett's expression tells me otherwise. And if that isn't enough, his next comment tells me I've fucked up.

"Now that I know you're safe, I'm going to head out. I'm not really wanted here anyway."

I flinch like he has hit me, which I immediately regret. Why am I so worried about what he thinks?

Garett cuts off my internal battle by striding over to me and enveloping me in a bear hug. I wonder if this is where the term 'bear hug' comes from. He gives great hugs. I immediately feel a little better, although I'm not going to admit that to anyone.

"I didn't mean it like that, Ari... I think we just... A bear shifter does not belong with a bunch of wolves. I'm needed back with my people. Call me if you need anything, okay?" At this last part he gently holds my chin, not letting go until I nod at his question.

Pulling away, he looks to Alexander and they do that male communication thing where they nod and grunt at each other. Whatever was communicated seems to be acceptable to Garett as he turns back to me, kissing my forehead gently before walking away.

"Well, that was dramatic," Seb comments and I glare at him, about to respond with a snarky comment when my phone buzzes in my hand. I completely forgot I even had it, what with

Garett distracting me. I quickly put in my passcode and grimace at the screen. Seventeen missed calls and 26 text messages, the last of which read:

Tori: CALL ME NOW, OR I AM SUMMONING SOME HELL HOUNDS AND COMING TO GET YO' ASS.

Oh shit. I'm in big trouble. I scroll through the other messages. Most of them are from Tori, although I'm surprised to see a few are from Eric, which get increasingly concerned as I didn't reply. I send off a quick reply.

Me: Hey Eric, sorry for the late reply, something came up. I'm fine, taking a break from the hospital for a while. I'll see you soon though.

With a sigh I look over at the men still in the room, Alexander propping up the wall in the corner, and Seb lounging on the bed like he owns it.

"I need to call my friend. This may take a while." I say this to try and get some privacy, but no, they just nod and stay where they are. Sighing again, I dial Tori's number.

After what feels like the longest phone call in history and many assurances to Tori that I am okay and not being held against my will, I hang up. Trying to convince your overprotective witch best friend that you're not being held captive turned out to be a challenge.

"But you have never wanted anything to do with the local pack before. I can keep you safe. I'll magic up a few 'friends' to keep you protected. We don't need them, Ari."

Her words are true, and I don't doubt that she could keep me safe. The problem? That would require dark magic, and Tori walks a very fine line with her magic already. I do not want to be responsible for pushing her over that line and turning her dark. Not to mention that using that kind of magic would bring ASP down on us like a tonne of bricks. No, this is the best solution for the moment. I will work here and travel back to the apartment at night. I will only shift when I am on Moon River territory, per their suggestions, and I will shift as little as I can get away with.

Glad that conversation is over with, for now at least, I glance down at my phone and see another message from Eric. Frowning, I click onto the message.

Eric: Are you safe? Do you need protection?

Well, that's confusing. I might have accepted the message if he was just asking if I was safe. I did disappear off the radar, after all. But to follow it up with do I need protection? Does he know more than he lets on? He is human – Tori would have told me otherwise – so why is he asking if I need protection like he knows what's been going on? Could he be one of the few humans that knows? I send him a message in return.

Me: What do you mean by that? I am safe.

Eric: Look, can we meet up? I have something I need to talk to
you about.

I sigh, rubbing at my eyes. Why can't anything be simple?
I'm about to reply when Alex comes stalking over, eyeing up
my phone.

"Everything okay?" he asks. Having eavesdropped on my
entire conversation with Tori, he obviously wants to know
what is going on in my text messages too. Nosy wolves.

"Yeah, just another complication. It's fine. What are you still
doing here, anyway? Don't you have important Beta business to
attend to?" I ask with maybe a little more snark than I had
intended, my eyes flashing with frustration.

Of course, Alex doesn't miss a thing and raises his eyebrows
at my lack of control. Luckily for him, he doesn't mention it.
Seb, on the other hand, has no problem making comments.

"Ari, they are going to rip you to shreds if you can't control
yourself tonight." Great. However, he is right – I need to get
control of myself.

"Come on Sebastian, let's leave Ari to get ready for tonight,"
Alexander says as he goes to leave the room. Just as he is
turning away, I remember something from my conversation
with Tori.

"Oh, Alex, did you or one of Moon River Pack go to my
apartment the other night?" They must have been one of the
'hotties' Tori kept referring to, trying to make the best of the
situation and hook me up with someone. My stomach sinks a
little as he shakes his head.

"No, we were ordered to stay away. The first contact we

have had with you was when I spoke to you at the bar the other night."

Shit. So who was this mysterious shifter that had turned up on my doorstep? Like I don't already have enough to deal with.

Alex is still waiting at the door expectantly for Seb, who shakes his head as he gets up and starts looking through the wardrobe in the borrowed room, muttering something about 'helping' me to get ready. I share a bemused look with Alexander and wave him out of the room. I had hoped for a bit of quiet to sort through my thoughts. I am so used to being by myself that having all these people around me, who actually *want* to be around me, is a little overwhelming. But as Seb picks up the horrendous pink dress from earlier and models it against his muscular chest, making me double over with laughter, I find myself thinking that perhaps that isn't such a bad thing.

Chapter Seven

Turns out that Seb's idea of helping me to get ready is very different to my idea. However, I have never laughed as much as I have in this last hour, my cheeks aching from smiling too much. I don't make friends easily. Sure, I can talk to people at work and care for my patients and their relatives – building a rapport is important in my profession. But in my personal life, I like to keep to myself.

I had always been alone until Tori came barrelling into my life, and I couldn't have turned away her friendship even if I had wanted to. She is like me – isolated and different from her kind – which is why we stick up for one another. She is the closest thing to family that I have.

Garett is the only other person I would consider a true friend. We met when Tori was taking me 'out on the town' at the start of our friendship. I was still bewildered by the large city, with all the sounds, smells and people. It was so different to the small British town where I grew up, not that I had seen much of it, having been kept in isolation for so long. Having only just turned eighteen when I flew to America, I had not tasted alcohol before. Turns out the rules in the shifter community are more lenient than the American laws on alcohol. As shifters, we have a higher tolerance and it takes much more to get us drunk than humans. What I wasn't warned about was the

Fae drinks. Those are lethal. Feeling high as a kite after my first one and just about to accept a second from a very attractive Summer Fae, Garett intervened, saving me from a nasty headache and some very unpleasant side effects. I later discovered that Fae drinks bring our animals closer to the surface. Problem with that? It leaves shifters stuck in half-animal forms. Not nice.

Ever since that night, a tentative friendship has developed as he helped me adjust to being a lone wolf in the city, showing me the best places to shift. Tori is amazing, and I will always be grateful to her for what she has done for me, but she isn't a shifter. She will readily agree with this, and is always trying to get me to expand my social circle.

Seb pulls me out of my musing by wolf-whistling as I stand in front of the mirror. I glance across at my new friend and grin. He has a way of making me feel at ease. Sure, he flirts like it's going out of fashion, but I know he won't push me for anything like so many male shifters do. There is also no domination battles with him; he doesn't care that I am stronger. Glancing back to the mirror, I focus on my reflection and have to agree with him. I don't look half bad. I have settled on wearing the smart jeans and shirt that Alexander brought in. The jeans fit well, showing off my legs and ass nicely, with some little black boots that Seb stole from somewhere. The top is a white, over-sized ladies' shirt, which cinches in at the waist with a small brown belt. With the top two buttons undone, it shows off a little cleavage, and the belt accentuates my shape nicely. After I showered I left my hair to air-dry, so it falls in natural waves to just below my collarbone. I don't have any make-up with me, but I rarely wear any so I don't feel like I'm lacking anything.

Turning around, I smile at Seb and walk to the bed, where I

left Garett's leather jacket. Picking it up, I slide my arms into it as I walk towards the door, feeling comforted as the leather surrounds me.

"You can not wear another man's jacket to a shifter social," says Seb. "Especially not a Bear shifter. They will think you belong to him."

I stop in my tracks. "I don't give a flying fuck what they think. I don't belong to anyone. Not Garett. Not the pack," I fume, my walls slamming back in place. I hadn't even realised I had let them slip; I need to be more careful. Seems I can't escape from judgemental shifter thoughts.

"Woah girl. I wasn't saying you were, I'm just telling you what they are going to think if you walk into your presentation to the pack wearing the jacket of a Bear shifter. You may not like it, but gossip travels fast and you're a powerful, unattached, unmated female. People are going to want to know you, and if you go barrelling in there in that jacket and with the 'fuck off' expression you currently have on your face, it is not going to give a good impression," Seb explains, walking slowly towards me with his hands out to the side like he is taming a wild beast. Maybe that's what I am?

"What impression do I want to give them?" I ask tentatively. I don't even know. I am in uncharted territory. I don't want to join this pack, but I have an opportunity to interact with my own kind. "I don't have the best track record with packs," I say, not liking how vulnerable my voice sounds.

Without a word, Seb walks up to me and wraps his arms around me. I stiffen slightly at the sudden contact. Seb must feel it, but he doesn't mention it, just rubs my back softly. I relax ever so slightly into his arms. This is... nice. I breathe in his vanilla scent.

"Just be yourself. Give the pack a chance. They are a good lot."

I feel his voice rumble through his chest where I have rested my hand. His t-shirt is thin and I can feel his muscles shift as he rubs my back. I move my hand slowly over his chest and relax further into the embrace. I freeze as I feel a hardness press against me. Seb clears his throat and shifts his weight slightly and I bury my face into his chest to prevent him from moving away, worried that I am going to lose a friendship that has only just begun.

"I could really do with a friend right now, Seb," I mumble into his chest.

Pulling away from me, he gently takes hold of my chin and lifts it so my eyes meet his. They are soft, understanding.

"And that's exactly what you've got." He then winks at me, his usually cheeky look returning to his face. "I can't help it when I've got a beautiful woman pressed up against me."

I laugh and step away from him, feeling reassured, although I'm not completely sure what just passed between us.

Reluctantly I pull Garett's jacket off and drop it on the bed. I may not be trying to make a good impression here, but I shouldn't actively try to piss them off.

Straightening my shoulders, I prepare myself for what I may face this evening. Thankfully my wounds are pretty much healed, so other than stiff legs and a sore shoulder, you wouldn't know I had been so badly injured only the night before. All thanks to a naked puppy pile of guys. Who'd have thought it? Confident, strong, but non-threatening is the look I am going for. Let's hope it works.

"Let's do this."

Chapter Eight

In the middle of the compound, just behind the main house, is the 'hang-out', the building where they hold the socials. As we walk into the large lodge-type building, I see a room off to the left that is full of comfy looking sofas and beanbags in front of a large flat screen TV, with a couple of pool tables at the back of the room. Inside the main room there is a bar to one side – I'm guessing I will be spending a lot of my time there. There are tables set up all along one edge of the room, all of which are overflowing with food. The middle of the room is empty, I'm assuming for mingling and dancing, as I spy a DJ in the corner.

This seems more like a party than the social I was imagining it to be. The only socials I have been to in the past are Pack meetings, where everyone sat in silence listening to the Alpha. Those were certainly never anything to look forward to, whereas the atmosphere here is electric, an excited feeling coming off the pack members who walk past me. There are a few curious looks, a couple appraising, as if to gauge my strength, but nothing threatening and no fearful gazes. Very different to what I am used to.

The room is starting to fill now, the buzzing of voices rising in volume. The sight of smiling faces and hugs of reuniting friends and family makes a small part of me ache. I haven't felt that part of me in a long time. I push it away. I am fine. I have Tori and Garett. I don't need this.

As if sensing my walls reinforcing and the bricks re-cementing, Seb grabs onto my hand with a smile and pulls me through the crowd. I see a blonde blur before something barrels into me hard. Almost as quick as it happens, Seb is wrestling with a small, very excited child.

"Is this her? Is this her?" she asks, barely able to control her excitement before escaping from Seb's arms and launching herself at me again.

I barely catch her in time, and laugh at the giggling child in my arms. I raise a questioning eyebrow at Seb. It's clear to see that they are related: they both have the same messy blond hair and crystal-clear blue eyes.

"Jessica. You must stop throwing yourself at people, even if they are your brother's friends. I swear, one of these days..." An exasperated voice trails off behind me and I turn around to see an older version of the little girl in my arms.

A little plump, with a large bosom, she looks like all the mums in the storybooks I used to read when I was a child, before I was removed from the schooling system. So this must be Seb's mum. And the squirming child in my arms must be his sister. Giggling, Jessica jumps out of my arms and runs over to her mother, talking around a hundred words a minute about Seb's 'new friend'.

I look over at him, smiling at his expression as he watches his younger sister and mum.

"So, you told your family about me. Don't you think we're moving a little fast in our relationship?" I say with a teasing grin. After all, we only met this morning – with his naked body curled around mine. Ahem. I hope he left that part out when he spoke to his parents.

"What can I say? I wanted you to meet them. They know you're here to help the pack and wanted to meet you," he says with a grin, and then leans forward like he is sharing a secret. "You're a bit of a celebrity. We never get new wolves here."

Fantastic.

I see Alpha Mortlock and Lena step up onto a small stage at the front of the room, Lena gesturing for me to join them. I glance back to Seb and his family.

"Off you go, dear. We will be here once you are done. We can chat more then," Seb's mum tells me with a smile while trying, and failing, to tame Jessica's wild hair.

Seb nudges my shoulder and motions for me to head to the front of the room. Internally I sigh. Here we go.

Around me, people move out of my way, allowing me to walk to the front. Alexander and Isa are there too, the latter of whom nods her head to me in greeting. I am unsure where to stand, acutely aware that I can cause grave offence if I position myself in the wrong place. If I were to stand before Alexander or Isa, I would be disrespecting them by saying that I think I am stronger than both of them, whereas if I automatically place myself at the end I would be saying that I am weaker than them. As an outsider to the pack, it's not clear where I should be, as I don't really fit in anywhere.

Thankfully Alpha Mortlock saves me from having to decide as he calls me up onto the stage.

"Good evening, Moon River Pack. It is wonderful to see so many of you here tonight. Tonight is a special occasion, as we welcome a guest to our pack." There is a ripple of noise from the crowd, and I can guess that it's because I have been named a guest and not a new pack member.

"Ariana here will be our new nurse for a few months. She will be travelling here to care for you, so I ask that you show her the same respect as any other member of the pack. She is under pack protection, so any threat to her life is a threat to all of us. Is that understood?"

His last statement is said with the power of the Alpha behind his voice. I notice several heads bow low and a chorus of "Yes, Alpha" can be heard from the crowd. At this confirmation Alpha Mortlock smiles, the tension in the room dropping.

"Then make her feel welcome. Maybe we can convince her to join us. Now – enjoy, have fun!" he says, with a wink towards me. I smile back at him and step off the stage with a sinking feeling in my stomach. Now he has voiced his intentions to the whole pack, he wants me to join, which means that this is not going to be easy.

Isa walks up to me and gestures to a line of people waiting to meet me. And so it begins. I look around for Seb, but I can't see him anywhere. Alexander appears next to my shoulder, so I am surrounded by the Beta and Gamma of the pack. Appearances must be kept, I guess.

"If you're looking for Sebastian, you won't see him for a while. You're to meet the strongest, most important members of the pack," he informs me. I just look at him, gobsmacked.

"Bullshit," I say loudly, startling both Isa and Alexander. "Being important has nothing to do with power." Bloody pack politics getting in the way. "Where is he?" I demand. Alexander places a placating hand on my arm and I glare at it.

"You won't be helping him by doing this. You will be putting a target on his back."

I growl quietly under my breath, my frustration causing my control of my power to slip, making the wolves near me pay closer attention. I have just announced how powerful I am, and now I have them eyeing me up like I am a shiny new toy. *Suck it up, Ari. You can't change centuries' worth of pack politics overnight.*

And so begins the tedious procession of all the 'important' members of the pack. Thankfully there aren't too many of them, and I find myself actually liking a few of them. We reach the end of the line and I sigh with relief. Maybe I can go and enjoy myself now. Isa stiffens and mutters something under her breath in German, which I'm pretty sure is a curse word. I follow her gaze and it's all I can do to stop my jaw from falling open.

Stalking towards me like I am his next meal is the most gorgeous man I have ever seen. He must be just over six foot, and looks like he was a warrior in a past life. He has a vicious scar that runs down the side of his face, which only adds to the impression, and his stormy grey eyes stare out at me. His face is in a frown, his lips tight as he comes closer towards me and I get the impression that he doesn't smile all that often. I can think of a few activities that could change that... *Behave, Ari! Not the right time or place.*

Unlike the others, I can feel the Alpha power rolling off him, and I'm unsure why Alpha Mortlock would have such a strong wolf here who wasn't in a position of power. He feels danger-ous. If I know what's good for me, I need to stay away from him. Unfortunately, my wolf thinks the opposite. I feel her brush up against my barriers, pushing our power out to meet his. I see his eyes widen as it hits him, stopping him in his tracks. His face twists into a snarl.

"Stay away from me, Shadowborn. Nothing good can happen from having you here," he spits out, before spinning on his heels and leaving the hall.

Well. That was pleasant. I look to Isa, who is shaking her head, then over to Alexander, who looks like he is having to stop himself from following the rude stranger.

"That is Killian. I would avoid him if you can," is all the

explanation I get from Alexander before he walks away. I guess I am going to have to do my own research there, then.

Isa makes her excuses and walks over to a group of other shifters who are taking loudly in German.

I look around me. Everyone is with their friends and family. They all seem... happy. For the first time, I feel lonely, like the life I lead may be lacking. I never knew what that was before, but maybe this is it.

Pushing these confusing feelings aside, I use this time to find Seb. He is in the corner of the room with a plate piled high with food, chatting to one of the men from this morning. Seb's mother, who I have learnt was called Gloria, is sitting at one of the tables watching fondly as Jessica plays with some of the other children. I sit with her and she smiles at me, petting my hand.

"How are you finding your first pack social?" she asks, with a knowing look on her face.

"A little overwhelming, to be honest. There are so many people here. But, it's not what I expected. Everyone is happy," I comment as I look around the room, taking in all the sights.

Raising her eyebrows, Gloria tilts her head as she looks at me, her eyes seeing more that I would like.

"Why wouldn't they be happy, dear? They are safe and protected here, surrounded by those who love them."

"That must be nice," I reply quietly. I don't really mean to say it out loud, and I say it more to myself than to Gloria. However, I see her nod to herself, like she has come to a conclusion. I lean back in my seat, watching those around us. Seb keeps glancing at me when he thinks I'm not looking.

"So, what's the deal with Killian?" I ask Gloria. She seems like the kind of woman who would know everyone in the pack.

Seb wanders over with his friend, and they pull up chairs next to us.

"He is complicated, that one. He was Alpha of one of the largest packs in New York. There was an attack on his pack," Gloria explains, her voice heavy with sorrow. I remember hearing of that attack, several years ago. I thought the whole pack had been wiped out.

"He screwed up. He's the reason that his pack is dead. There was some sort of agreement with Alpha Mortlock, and he allowed him to come here. Fucking bad idea, if you ask me. He is a cold bastard who doesn't belong here," Seb's friend chips in.

His view seems kind of harsh to me, but I see Seb nodding. That explains why someone who is so strong isn't in a position of power. I can't imagine how difficult it is to go from Alpha of a successful pack to an outsider in a pack that doesn't really want you there. Well, I know all about the outsider bit.

"He is okay. Bit of a bastard, but considering what he went through, I can understand that. Steve here is right, though, he doesn't fit in here, and he makes no effort to. I would try and stay away from him if you can," Seb offers.

I look at the guy next to Seb – Steve, I am assuming. Steve uses our eye contact as an excuse to start a conversation.

We spend the next ten minutes or so chatting about the pack, the social, what I enjoy doing outside of work, until the DJ starts playing music. Several couples go up and start danc- ing, and I notice Alpha Mortlock and Lena dancing away up near the front. Seb drags me to my feet, pulling me onto the dance floor, ignoring my protests.

Despite what I thought, I find I'm actually enjoying myself. I have a dance with Seb, Gloria and Jessica, a couple with Steve and even one with Alpha Mortlock. I just finish a particularly vigorous dance with Seb that has me in fits of laughter – his dance style is… unusual – when I bump into Alex. I literally fall into his arms.

"You don't have to throw yourself at me to get me to dance with you," he comments with a grin.

"Yeah, you wish, Casanova. Since when do you dance? I've seen you propping up the wall over there like it couldn't stand on its own. I thought you were allergic to fun?" I tease.

It's true, though. So far this evening I have only seen him watching everyone else, always on duty. He leans in closer to me as the DJ changes the music, a slower song coming on. People around us couple up and start to slow-dance. Placing his hands on my lower back, he pulls me so I'm almost pressed against him. I place my hand on his chest to stop our bodies from touching. He uses this as an invitation to start moving us to the music. I'm really not a dancer, so it's more of a sway.

"So, you've been watching me, then," he says softly in my ear, saying it sounds more like a statement than a question.

I snort. Of course I have been watching him; he makes me nervous.

"Don't flatter yourself, buddy. I watch everyone." And that's the truth. In fact, I am watching everyone as we dance now, taking in details, looking out for anyone who is paying too much attention.

Alexander raises his eyebrows and stops dancing.

"Do you always push everyone away, or is it just me?" he asks. His tone is soft, like he is asking a normal question, but his body language is tense.

I stare at him, gobsmacked. Where has this come from? I do my best fish impression, lost for words about what to say.

"And are you always this rude?" I finally retort, feeling my temper rise as we stare at each other.

Alexander has obviously reached his limit as well as,

without a word, he turns heel and leaves the room. It's at this point that I notice the room has gone silent. Everyone has stopped to watch the show.

"Wow, Ari, you sure know how to liven up a party!" Seb comments loudly, causing chuckles around us. Thankfully people start dancing again, only throwing me curious glances rather than full-on stares.

Pulling me to one side, he puts an arm around me, lowering his voice.

"You okay?" he asks, and I hate the look of concern in his eyes.

"I'm fine, Seb," I say, shaking his arm off me before grabbing his hand. "Let's go dance."

The next hour or so I spend dancing to try and forget my embarrassing moment with Alex. I don't want to think about it now, or about the reasons why Alex might care if I let people get close to me. I have a couple of drinks, and Gloria keeps trying to feed me. Jessica seems to have taken a liking to me, and the rest of the pack seem to dote on her. To be honest, it's easy to see why. Wolves have always been protective of their young, but happiness just seems to shine from her. One of the grumpy pack Elders is currently having his shoulder-length hair braided by her, and although he is scowling I think he secretly likes it.

I'm chatting to one of Seb's friends when a heavy hand grips my shoulder. Startled, I spin to face the person touching me, a snarl on my lips. A tall male puts his hands up in a peaceful gesture, but his smile is anything but nice.

"Hey there, pretty lady, no harm meant. I just want to talk with you. Care to dance?" he asks, and I get the feeling he is used to getting his own way. Normally I would never give this kind of guy the time of day, but I have agreed to try and integrate into the pack while I am here, so reluctantly I nod.

Ignoring his outstretched hand, I walk onto the dance floor, waiting for him to join me. Immediately he pulls me in close, and my hackles rise as I push back against his chest a little to gain some space. Presumptuous much? I study the man before me. He is good looking, I guess, but he is full of himself, which is a major turn-off.

"So, what is someone as strong as you doing with the runts of the pack?" He removes his arm from my lower back and gestures towards Seb, Gloria and the group of shifters I have been spending the evening with. "You should be spending your time where you belong, with the strongest of the pack. With a male who can keep up with you."

Nope. I know what I promised the Alpha, but I am not putting up with an attitude like that. I may have just met those people, but they have already shown me more kindness in the last few hours than I've experienced in my life. Grabbing onto his shirt, I pull him closer, obviously startling him with my show of strength.

"Listen, shit for brains. If the strongest in the pack are anything like you, I want nothing to do with them. No one tells me where my place is. Those people over there that you talk down about? They have treated me better than anyone ever has, and are probably more decent than you could ever hope to be."

So maybe I am a little strong with my words, but every single one is true. I shove him away from me and start to walk back to Seb and his friends. Limp dick obviously doesn't get the message as he grabs my arm and spins me around.

"Now listen here, you little bitch–" he starts, his face getting red with rage, obviously not used to being spoken to that way. I interrupt him, putting an end to his useless tirade with a low blow.

"Did you not hear me? Leave me the fuck alone. I would rather eat garbage than spend another minute with you."

I probably shouldn't be provoking a shifter who is shaking with rage, but I won't let people talk about my friends that way. I catch myself at the use of the words 'friends' and realise that it's true. In such a short space of time I have come to appreciate the familial group I've spent time with today. Walking away, I see the gratitude on Gloria's face, although when I look at Seb he seems worried.

"Ari..." he warns, before a deafening roar fills the room, filling me with dread. That's a sound I know all too well. Someone just lost their temper and conceded the battle with their wolf.

"I CHALLENGE YOU!" bellows across the room, and for the second time that evening everyone goes silent. I turn around to see who has been challenged, but the lead in my stomach already knows.

Panting like he has just run a marathon is the supreme dick-head who felt he had a claim on me. His eyes, glowing an unearthly green, have turned fully wolf, and at the end of his fingers his nails have turned to claws – sharp, wicked-looking points that can slice open a person in seconds. Claws that are aimed right at me.

Oh, shit.

Chapter Nine

Mutters and whispers fill the air around me, and I hear mentions of 'not allowed' and 'guest'. Dread fills my stomach. I may not know much about how packs work, but even I know that formal challenges can't be turned down. If I forfeit, then I am subjected to the same punishment as losing a challenge: death. That is not an option for me. I have overcome too much to get to this point only to have to give it up all because I have damaged some idiot's pride.

Seb pulls me from my thoughts as he pushes through the crowd and tries to stand in front of me.

"Marcus, you can't challenge her. She is a guest of the pack," he states, and I can hear the fury in his voice, very out of character from the usual fun-loving Seb that I have come to know.

Turns out that dickhead, or Marcus as he is apparently called, doesn't like being told what he can and can't do. Snarling, he leaps forward, slashing at Seb with his semi-turned hand, razor-sharp claws slicing across his chest. I hear someone cry out – I think it's Gloria, but in my rage-filled mind I'm not sure, since my focus is entirely on Marcus.

Stepping in front of a crouched Seb, I move into a protective stance in case Marcus dares to attack him again. I have hurt many in the past, more than I care to think about, and I promised myself that I would never hurt anyone again when I left my old pack. I'm trying to make a better life for myself, to atone for the actions of my past, which is why I took a vow to do no harm when I trained to be a nurse and help people for a living. But, right now, all I can think about is the fact that this bastard has hurt someone I care for.

My wolf rushes to the surface and I feel her walking under my skin. We are in complete agreement for once, wanting to protect Seb and make the bastard that hurt him pay. Mutters fill the room again as our power fills it, pushing against each other. Some of the weaker shifters are forced to their knees, a few even bursting into their wolf form, and crouch against the floor in submission against our warring energies. The power is so thick in the room you could choke on it.

"I accept," I pronounce, in a voice that I hardly recognise as my own as I take a step towards him.

"Ari, no. Don't do this," I hear Seb's pain-laced voice plead.

I glance over my shoulder at him, not trusting Marcus enough to turn my back on him. Seb is leaning against one of the chairs, Gloria and a couple of other shifters with him. I can see that the wound isn't too deep, since it has stopped bleeding already. He should heal quickly, although, as it has been caused by another shifter, it will probably scar. My nursing side is satisfied that he will be okay while I deal with this threat. I smile in what I hope is a reassuring way, but I'm pretty sure it appears as a grimace and turn back to the problem at hand.

I'm still not fully healed from the attack last night, and here I am about to engage in a challenge to the death with a fully grown male shifter. I must be out of my fucking mind.

I hear a commotion and when I look over to where the sound is coming from I see Alpha Mortlock moving through the crowd. Looking furious, he storms towards Marcus, grabbing him by the shoulders as if he is going to shake some sense into him.

"How dare you issue a challenge to a guest? You know the rules. Rescind your challenge immediately," he orders, the full power of the Alpha evident in his command.

Man, I wouldn't want to be Marcus right now. I can see his face contort in pain as he fights against the command, his muscles trembling. He may be strong, but he's not Alpha strong. A sliver of hope flares to life in me as I think there may be a way out of this. I am not scared, but I am practical, and entering into a fight you are not sure you can win is foolish. Wolf Ari does not agree, and I know she wants to rip the shit out of Marcus. But thankfully for me, right now I'm in charge of this shitshow.

However, that sliver of hope is shot down by Marcus's next comment.

"Too late, Alpha. She already accepted," he grinds out, a grin of sick satisfaction across his smarmy face.

Alpha Mortlock turns to me, his face grim. "Is this true?" he asks, his voice resigned.

I nod. Some of the wolves who have gathered around Marcus are shouting out that now I have accepted the challenge, the Alpha has to honour it. I guess Marcus has his own cheerleaders. I nearly smirk at the image of the large, buff shifters in little cheerleading costumes. *Come on, brain, not the right time. Focus.*

Alpha Mortlock sighs and nods towards Marcus. He turns to address the crowd.

"Marcus of Moon River Pack has challenged Ariana, lone wolf and guest of Moon River Pack. As the challenge has been accepted, I have no choice but to allow this to proceed. But I do not condone this and there will be consequences," he says sternly to the watching shifters.

The crowd erupts into shouts, many, I am pleased to hear, who are protesting the challenge.

"Enough! I have made my decision," he shouts before walking to me. Pulling me aside, he lowers his voice. "Do you know the rules? You know what you're getting into?"

I nod. Anyone in the pack can issue a formal challenge. Usually it is used when a shifter wishes to change their station, because they want a higher role within the pack. Shifters can also issue challenges to someone they believe has wronged them, however, as a fight to the death, it's not something that happens often. You wouldn't challenge someone for crushing your roses, for example. Apparently it's against the rules to challenge a guest, but once the challenge has been accepted, it cannot be overturned, not even by the Alpha – who knew? No weapons are allowed other than claws or fangs. Most fights begin in wolf form, but some prefer to start in human form.

"Prepare yourself," he says loudly to everyone, but I feel like he is directing this comment at me.

The crowd steps back, creating a loose circle around us, with me at one end and Marcus at the other. A group of people has formed at his end. I assume they are his supporters, given the sneers and growls they are throwing my way.

I hear a commotion behind me and turn to find I have a large group of people who have come to support me or offer me words of guidance, some of whom I have never spoken to before. A small part of my heart hurts at this show of community, that people who I don't even know are willing to support me through this. I do notice that Alexander hasn't returned to the room, and a part of me is disappointed. Gloria pushes through and places a hand against my cheek.

"You show that nasty brute," she remarks, which brings a smile to my face.

I take a step forward into the makeshift ring and start shrugging off my top, indicating that I will start in wolf form. I don't trust myself to shift quickly enough if I need to later on in the fight. Alpha Mortlock barks out for everyone to turn while I shift. As one, the whole room turns, all except Marcus, who smirks at me, crossing his arms and daring me with his eyes to strip in front of him.

Fuck him. Standing tall, I remove the rest of my clothes, meeting Marcus's eyes as I do it. I will not let him make me feel ashamed or cowed into covering myself. I am not his victim; I am no one's victim. Once I finish undressing, I crouch to the ground and call my wolf to the surface. She rushes out all at once, ready for justice.

The shift takes longer than I would like, unpractised as I am since I am still avoiding shifting unless absolutely necessary. Once I'm in wolf form I get to all fours and snarl at Marcus, who smirks and bursts into wolf form within twenty seconds, not even bothering to take his clothes off. Show off. The crowd turns back around and I feel the anticipation, which is thick in the air as they watch the two of us. However, I feel more nervous tension in the room than I was expecting, and I almost wonder if they are worried about my well-being.

I can hear Seb's voice as he demands to be let closer. I'm distracted and I turn to look at him, my need to check he is okay overwhelming my need for revenge. Marcus uses this moment of distraction to charge at me.

Fuck, he is big!

Thankfully, this should make him slower and I dart out of the way, snarling at him as he flies past me. I lower myself into a defensive position as he circles me. He goes to attack my right, so I instinctively move to the left, unfortunately realising too late that he's tricked me and I dive into his jaws. With a sickening crunch they sink into my already injured shoulder. I howl in pain as he shakes his jaw, his fangs ripping into the newly healed muscles and tendons. With a final shake he lets go of my shoulder, sending me flying into a table. Pain flares through my back at the impact, although compared to the agony of my shoulder it's nothing.

I haul myself to my feet, limping as I try to avoid putting any extra weight on my injured shoulder. Distracted by the pain I don't see Marcus until it's too late, and he bites down onto my hind leg, in the exact place where I had been injured the day before. I snarl as his plan becomes clear. The bastard is deliberately aiming for places he knows are going to cause me the most pain. He is playing with me, trying to maim me and cause as much agony as he can before he makes the killing blow. I turn, my leg slicing more in his jaws as I swipe at his belly with my claws. I also manage to bite down on his flank in the process, causing him to let go of me and retreat to the other side of the ring.

I try to back up and feel my legs give way. I shouldn't be fighting this soon after being injured. Besides, I'm not exactly the best at fighting in my wolf form. My wolf whines in pain, and I hear a scuffle behind me as Seb demands that this be called off and I hear shouts of agreement and calls of this being 'inhumane'. Surprise shoots through me. This pack acts very differently from what I expected. Alpha Mortlock looks on, but he is unable to intervene now. He has to stay impartial, although I can tell he wants to wade in and stop this.

"Get up," I hear a command.

I turn my head, my ears flat against my skull, my lips pulled back over my jaw in a snarl. If I wasn't in so much pain I would be surprised that Killian is crouched next to me. He is sneering at me, looking at me like I deserve the treatment I am receiving, but I see something like fear in his eyes. I must be delirious with pain. I growl at him, telling him to back off.

"Useless," he spits at me, causing anger to swell inside me. Can't he just leave me alone?

"Do you want to die? No? Then get. The. Fuck. Up," he commands, his Alpha power flowing through me, giving me strength. I am so tired, but he is right. That pisses me off. I am not going to die here today, especially not at the jaws of a scumbag like Marcus.

Pushing up on trembling legs, I turn to face Marcus. It was foolish letting my guard down. He could have attacked me. Luckily he is struggling as well, but I'm losing energy fast and I need to end this quickly.

"Use your brains. You can't have survived this long as a Shadowborn without them," Killian chides.

I don't understand why he is helping me. I'm pretty sure he can't stand the sight of me. But the anger that fills me at his comments pushes away the fog of pain that is making it difficult to think. Perhaps that was his plan after all? I don't have time to think about it, though, as Marcus prowls towards me again. I start to analyse the wolf in front of me and play over the last few attacks. I need to look for his weaknesses.

"Show him what happens when you fuck with a Shadowborn," Killian whispers, and my wolf agrees with him.

I go into a defensive stance, favouring my uninjured leg. Marcus picks up his pace, running towards me with his jaws wide. I stay still. Just as he is about to attack me I see it: he has left his neck undefended.

I pounce with a growl and lock my teeth into his neck. Twisting, I pull him down and, with my fangs in his jugular, he has no choice but to follow me. I twist again so I'm on top. I have the upper hand. All I need to do now is squeeze, but I hesitate as a memory surfaces.

His eyes widen as my jaws tighten against his neck. So young. He doesn't deserve to lose his life.

"Ari. Do it. Now." A crack of a whip in the background makes me flinch, his voice echoing in my ears. I bite down, quickly and without mercy. I feel his neck break under my fangs, and watch as the light leaves his terrified eyes. They stare at me and his last words echo in my ears: "Why?" And I know this day will haunt me.

I hear him step closer, his shoes clicking against the floor, and I flinch as his hand falls on my shoulder.

"Well done, little wolf."

I shudder as the memory overcomes me. I hear my name being shouted, and shouts to end it. I glance down and see fear in Marcus's eyes. He closes them as he prepares to lose his life.

No.

My wolf fights against me, but in this, I am absolute. I will not take another life. Closing my eyes I summon my human body. Crouched and naked, I place my human hand onto Marcus's bleeding neck. I squeeze enough that he opens his eyes. They widen in shock. Before he can get any ideas I call my shadow form, not to change fully, not enough for anyone else to see. But enough to scare the shit out of Marcus.

"Do you concede?" I ask, my voice more wolf than human. I shift only my hand, so it sinks slowly into his neck, then I reform it enough that he can feel the pressure there.

He nods, eyes wide.

"Stay down," I command, putting my full Alpha power into my voice.

He whines. I stand as well as I can on my injured leg, not ashamed of my nakedness.

"I will not kill him," I say to Alpha Mortlock, but loud enough that the rest of the pack can hear me.

The Alpha nods at me, announcing my victory. I am surrounded by people, congratulating me, checking my wounds, admiring my decision. All of this passes in a blur, as my mind is elsewhere and my body goes through the motions. I look through the crowd, searching for someone who wasn't there. It's not until I can't see him that I realise I am disappointed that Alex isn't here to congratulate me. It isn't until I am escorted from the hall that I realised that Killian was no longer in the room.

Chapter Ten

For the second morning in a row I wake up with Seb's naked body pressed up against me, but probably not in the way that he hoped when I insisted he share my bed. Alpha Mortlock wanted to use his puppy-pile method again, but I refused, and in my pain-addled state I hadn't let anyone close to Seb. He had protested, saying he was fine, but until I was able to check him over and see for myself, I wouldn't let anyone near me to look at my wounds.

I spent the night with him wrapped around me, unable to sleep, twitching at every sound in the unfamiliar room. I don't know why I'm acting this way with Seb, but something about him sets off my protective instincts. At some point I must have fallen asleep, as I wake up with his arms around me. I stay still so I don't wake him. It's nice, being held purely because someone wants to hold me: no ulterior motives, nothing in it for him, other than for comfort.

He moves in his sleep and I feel his erection pressed up against me. This wakes me up fully. It also wakes up my lady parts, making me squirm. *Now is not the time, traitorous body.* I can feel Seb wake up, as he nuzzles his face into my neck. I can also feel when he senses my arousal, damn the shifter sense of smell. Taking a deep breath, which comes out as a predatory growl, he runs his hands over my hips. I arch back into his body, unable to stop myself from reacting to his touch. We are in dangerous territory here. It would be so easy to cross that line. All I need to do is roll over and kiss him.

I stop moving. All the past romantic dalliances have been just that. Dalliances. They are great, but they all come to an end very quickly. Am I willing to lose this new friendship because I'm horny and can't keep it in my pants? Considering my reaction last night when Seb was hurt, I'm going to say no. We may not have known each other for long, but my protective instincts are on overdrive with him, and I'm not sure I could cope if anything happened to him.

Seb, having felt me stop moving, also stops, waiting for my lead, but I can hear his heavy breathing behind me. I scrunch up my eyes. I can't believe I'm turning away a gorgeous guy who obviously wants to spend the morning getting to know me in the biblical sense.

"Seb," I say with a sigh, regret clear in my voice.

He instantly rolls away from me and I look over my shoulder to see him getting out of bed, pulling on his jeans. Panic bolts through me and I bolt upright in bed, the covers falling around my waist exposing my chest.

"Wait, where are you going?" I ask.

He turns and smiles at what he sees. "I'm going to take a cold shower. It's rude to have a hard-on around your naked best friend," he replies with a wink.

Relief fills me and I lay back in the bed with a laugh.

Now that I'm alone, I think over the events of the night before. I roll my shoulder. It's sore and stiff, but when I look at it I just see the slightly raised pink skin of new scars. I look at my legs, expecting to see mangled skin, but I'm greeted with the same sight as my shoulder. New scars to add to the collection. It's a good thing I'm not vain. I've never been bothered by my scars; they show a battle that I have lived through, and they are the marks of a survivor. I wouldn't say I'm proud of them, and I don't go out of my way to show them off, but I'm certainly not ashamed of them.

I muse over the fact that I'm healing so quickly. Sure, we have fast healing times, but injuries caused by other shifters take longer to heal and, considering the damage that was done, especially as it was reinjuring a previous wound, I should be in far worse shape than I am. Seb's injuries practically healed before my eyes during the night as I watched him sleep. Perhaps it is to due to our friendship. Does the healing thing work better with people you are close to? I have to ask Alexander next time the growly Beta decides to show his face.

Urgh. The thought of having to leave this room and face everyone after last night is not something I want to deal with. Marcus is going to be a problem. The challenge is a fight to the death for a reason. Wolves can't stand a challenge to their honour, and Marcus is too much of a dick to let it stand that a woman defeated him. I've literally been on pack grounds for 24 hours and I'm already causing problems. I'm not blaming the pack – they have been nothing but welcoming, which is a massive blow to the feels. I hadn't expected the kindness shown by complete strangers to an outcast like me.

And now I have to go out there and help them, heal them. I feel their expectations on my shoulders like a heavy weight. It was okay when they were just nameless, faceless patients that I was dealing with, but now I know them, and even in this short time I have begun to care for them. I can see that if I stay here for much longer they will begin to care for me too. My breathing speeds up. Nothing good happens when people care for me. Tori is safe in the apartment and she has friends who would care for her. Garett can look after himself, and I have kept my distance up until now to keep him safe. Seb blindsided me with his instant friendship, but he is safe within the pack.

Now I have a whole group of people who are seeping their way into my cold, shrivelled little heart.

I jump to my feet, my battered body protesting at the speed of my movements. I start pulling on my clothes. I need to get out of here; I need space.

Glassy dead eyes stare back at me as I remove my jaws from around his neck.

I shake my head to clear it from the memories trying to flood my brain, but it creeps in again.

I step away from the freshly dead body, look behind me and jump from the corpse that lies next to me. Rather than a nameless body, I see the body of little Jessica. No – this isn't real. I didn't know Jessica then. I step back and startle as my foot touches a hand. Spinning around, I howl in grief as I look at the body of the boy I just murdered. It's not the nameless boy I played with, the boy who gave me comfort – it's Seb. His face is twisted, as if in terrible pain.

"It's your fault I'm dead."

I spin, my heart rate spiking in panic as I try to find who spoke. My eyes widen as I take in the room full of bodies: Alexander, Tori, Seb, Gloria, members of the pack whose names I don't even remember, all dead.

"Ari."

I snap out of my twisted flashback as I step back into a solid wall. Except walls aren't warm, and they don't wrap their arms around you. I stiffen, ready to break free of my captor's arms, until I take a deep breath. The scent of the woods, and the sweet smell of brandy reach me: Alex.

"Ari, breathe," he orders.

I do as commanded, trying to slow my breathing now that I know what happened in my 'memory' wasn't real. We stand there for a long while, his strong arms holding me up and I try to ground myself. The words 'they're alive' keep running through my head, my mantra to keep myself in the here and now.

"You want to tell me what's going on? I came to see you and I could sense your panic through the door. I thought something had happened," he admits.

I turn my head a bit and I can see that the door is now hanging off its hinges. He literally ripped the door off to get to me. Too much. This is too much.

I pull from his arms, gathering up my meagre belongings that have been strewn around the room.

"Ari, what's going on? Where are you going? If it's Marcus, he's been banished. You don't have to worry about him anymore."

I shake my head. Marcus is the least of my worries right now.

"I just need some space. I'll be back. I just need time, okay?" I blurt out, not looking him in the eye.

I hear him sigh, and out of the corner of my eye I see him nod.

"Tell Seb I'll see him around," I ask, before I start walking out of the room.

This place is like a bloody maze. I walk around the back of another building, looking for my car so I can get the hell out of here. Several people have tried to stop me to talk about last night, but I have just smiled tensely at them and walked on.

"Where the hell do you think you're going?" I hear shouted angrily at me.

I spin around and see a fuming Killian striding towards me. My temper boils, although my wolf perks up at the sight of him. *Down, girl.*

"And how is that any of your fucking business?" I demand, close to losing my temper. I am not in the mood for Mr. Dark and Moody to grow a conscience.

He snarls at me, and I can see his wolf is as close to the surface as mine. Our Alpha powers rub up against one another.

"It matters to me when you lose control and kill all of the wolves here. You're a fucking mess. It's a surprise you have survived this long as it is. You need to get yourself under control, before you cause any more problems," he goads me.

But he is right. I am going to get these wolves killed. I see a brief flash of panic in his eyes as he realises he isn't going to get the reaction he wanted. I turn away, my heart heavy, and restart trying to find my car.

"You're going to get yourself killed," he states. His voice is tinged with sadness as he says this.

I spin around, my temper flaring again. Why does he care if I get myself killed or not? He has made it clear that he thinks I am a danger to everyone around me. He clearly hates Shadow-born, so shouldn't my death please him?

"Why do you care what happens to me?" I demand, the fire back in my voice.

A look of confusion greets my question, like he doesn't have an answer. This disappears as his face hardens.

"Take your break. Once you've gotten over your pity party, come back and I'll teach you how a real wolf fights."

I snort at his comment, flipping him off as I turn away, stalking towards where I'm sure my bloody car is. What a dick. But, as I finally find my car and haul myself into it, I find that my heart isn't quite as heavy as it had been when I first left the house.

Chapter Eleven

I send Tori an SOS text and hightail it to the only place I can think of: Garett's bar. It's only 11 am, so the bar is dead when I walk in, only a few alcoholics nursing their morning drinks in the corner.

Garett is standing behind the bar, looking gorgeous in his tight uniform shirt and jeans. He smiles widely when he sees me, but this quickly turns to a scowl as he sees my slight limp and the look on my face.

"Someone hurt you," he states, his voice like granite, cold and hard.

I sigh, sliding into my favourite bar stool, my body protesting.

"I was challenged last night," I explain.

Cue lots of cursing and male grumbling. I watch in silence as Garett fights against his bear for control. It's quite a sight to see. He slowly, quietly, places the glass he was polishing onto the bar, bracing his arms against the bar like it is the only thing keeping him up. I reach across and grab the glass he was polishing, leaning over the bar to pour myself a whisky. Sure it is early for a drink, but cut me some slack – it has been one hell of a morning.

While I nurse my drink, Garett gets a co-worker to cover

the bar. Walking up to my side, he grabs my hand and pulls me along behind him.

"Come," he demands.

I follow him, not about to argue with a bear this close to losing control. I follow him up the stairs at the back of the bar, leading up to the apartment that he rents. It's handy living just above your workplace.

Pushing open the door, he holds it open for me. I duck under his arm and head into the apartment. It's nice in here: homey. It's not a large apartment, but it's big enough for Garett. I look around the room. I haven't been up here in a long time, but it looks the same. I walk over to the fireplace and there is a photo frame that takes a place of pride. I pick it up and surprise flashes through me as I realise it's a photo of me. I remember that day. Tori had decided that she needed to get to know my 'bear friend' better and had organised a picnic for the three of us. It had been a great day, but I don't remember this photo being taken.

I turn around to ask Garett where this has come from, but I stop at the expression I see there.

"Explain," he orders, his voice more bear than I have ever heard it.

So I do. I tell him about the events of the previous evening, I even tell him about me fleeing from the compound this morning.

"I just... They are all depending on me. I'm not good for any of them. It was okay when I didn't care for them or them for me. But now it's different. I already got Seb hurt. I'm going to get them all killed. I'm not good enough," I stumble out, all my pent-up feelings coming out in a rush.

"Ari, stop."

I look up, swallowing at the sight before me. Garett is

looking at me in a way I've never seen before. He prowls towards me, and I take a step back until I'm pressed up against a wall. He keeps walking until he is a fingerbreadth away from me. Placing his arms on the wall either side of me, blocking me in, I have no choice but to look up into his eyes. They are all bear at the moment, glowing back at me with his supernatural power. Seeing Garett like this awakens a different part of me, overshadowing my despair. Arousal spreads through me, and Garett makes a satisfied rumble as he scents it.

Pushing his hips up against me, I can feel his own arousal, hard and unyielding. My wolf, the hussy, is eager to reciprocate and I feel her walking under my skin. My eyes mirror his own.

"Never think that you aren't good enough. You are more than enough."

Lowering his head towards me, I can see in his eyes that he is waiting for me to make a move, and that he would back off if I asked him too. But I need this comfort right now. Sure, I have an attraction to another guy – ahem, a couple of other guys – but I need this physical comfort and I know Garett will do anything to protect me.

I lean forward, capturing his lips with my own. He groans into my mouth and we kiss, slow and unhurried as his hands begin to explore my body. I run my fingers over his chest, my nails scraping gently over his nipples as I trail them down towards his jeans. He bites down on my lower lip, pressing me further into the wall. I run my hand over the bulge in his jeans, before slipping them into his waistband. Feeling the velvet smoothness over the pure hardness of his cock is doing all sorts of things to my hormones, sending a shock of pure desire right to my core.

"I knew it!" someone shouts, causing me to jump.

Garett groans, dropping his head to my shoulder, but he

makes no effort to move. Standing on tiptoes, I peek over Garett's bulk and see a very smug Tori standing in the doorway. I pat at Garett's chest, signalling him to let me out. When he doesn't move, I duck out from under his arm, and he just rests his forehead against the wall in defeat.

Noticing Garett's demeanour, I raise my eyebrows at Tori, a smirk crossing my face.

"Bloody hell. Look what you've done to him," I remark as I embrace Tori.

Tori laughs, returning my hug tightly, holding on for a fraction longer than our usual slap on the back.

"Girl, this has nothing to do with me, and everything to do with your months of holding out on him." She saunters up to him and pats him on the shoulder. "Poor baby," she mocks.

My mouth drops open in mock outrage at her comment. Garett turns from his position against the wall and smiles at Tori. He doesn't try to hug her like I did, knowing that she has just as many issues over being touched as I do.

"Hey, witch," he calls out to her affectionately as he walks over to the sofa. I can't help but notice that he discreetly tries to reposition himself as he sits down.

Tori walks back towards the doorway where she had left some bags, which she brings over to the coffee table in the middle of the living room. Sitting opposite Garett, she begins unpacking the bags, which it turns out, are full of take-out food.

"Months," she says.

I make an ungraceful sound, which sounds suspiciously like a snort. Still stuck on her comment about finding the two of us getting hot and heavy against the wall. "This was a completely spur-of-the-moment thing. We were just letting off some tension after everything that happened. You know. Stress," I ramble. My voice sounds unconvincing even to me. "It's not going to happen again," I comment.

It wouldn't. No matter how much my wolf wanted to howl at that thought. Garett wouldn't want just a tumble in the sheets; he would want more from me than that. He wouldn't be able to help himself. It's in his nature to be protective.

I see Garett look up at my comment. I see a brief flash of hurt in his eyes, before he goes back to helping Tori unpack the food.

"Uh-huh," she comments, not for a minute sounding like she believes me. "Now will you stop deluding yourself and sit your ass down. The food is going cold. The food you promised to bring me *two nights* ago." She glares at me as she says this.

I cringe, knowing I'm in the wrong here. Bad friend award goes to me. It's not a good idea to piss off a witch, especially when it involves food.

I perch sheepishly on the end of the seat next to Garett, the only other available seat in the room. I don't want this to be awkward because I couldn't control my hormones. Besides, Garett deserves someone way better than me. For a start, I'm a wolf. He wouldn't ever be able to have a family with me. I'm not sure I would even want to start a family; I struggle to look after myself, let alone miniature versions of me.

I shudder at the thought. I wouldn't do that to him. Garett would make a good father, with his own cubs. He wouldn't have that with me.

Not to mention that I'm a hot mess. I don't mind a one-night fling, but a relationship is a whole new ball game. Within the supernatural community we are much more open and liberal with sex. We aren't squeamish about these things.

With Tori, Garett and now Seb, I have all I need. A small

part of me starts to call out that maybe that's not enough anymore. I crush that voice. I have all I need.

"I'm sorry, Tori, I've been a terrible friend. I just got so caught up in everything..." I trail off, feeling guilty.

If I weren't so used to looking out for myself, I would have thought to call her sooner. A normal, undamaged person would have done that.

It was a big shock to me when I first realised that another person cared for me. Our first major fight had been when I stayed out with a cute Fae and ended up on a little jaunt to the Fae realm. It had taken me a day and a half to find the portal back to the city. I found Tori pacing the apartment, in tears. It had left me bewildered that someone would be so upset because they were worried about where I was. I instantly went on the defensive, convinced she was mad at me because I had been out with a Fae. I think it was a shock to Tori as well, that she cared enough about someone that she had become so worried. Her past was almost as dark as mine.

I look up as I hear a rustling noise, a large grin spreading across my face.

"I was going to eat these in front of you and not let you have any, as punishment for putting me through hell. But I can't stay mad at that face," Tori teases, handing me a bag of doughnuts.

I greedily grasp at the doughnuts, clutching the sweet balls of heaven to my chest. I'm not a possessive person, but you better not even think about messing with my doughnuts.

"I love you," I tell her around a mouthful of the divine pastries.

She just laughs, knowing me well enough not to question the fact I'm eating dessert before the main course. Garett watches with a shake of his head, but I spot the small smile that crosses his lips.

"Right. Enough stalling. Tell me what's been going on," she demands.

I know better than to push her. With a sigh I explain the last few days.

When I finish retelling my story, Tori looks thoughtful. Pissed off, but thoughtful. Garett, on the other hand, looks ready to tear into someone. He has heard this all before, but listening to it again has set him off. Pacing up and down the room, he is beginning to give me a cramp in my neck from where I've been watching him.

"Alexander promised me you would be safe there. I never would have left you there if I thought you would have been in danger," he spits out, his voice tight with anger. His green eyes flash as his bear pushes to the surface. I'm surprised by his show of rage. He usually has very tight control over his bear, but the last couple of days I have never seen him closer to losing control.

"Well, I doubt he knew some asshole would challenge her. Besides, what idiot would accept that kind of challenge?" Tori comments, throwing a glare in my direction.

"I thought I had no choice but to accept!" I say indignantly.

They both ignore me and continue to talk about me as if I'm

not there. I decide to ignore them in return and tuck into the food. I'm not going to let good food go to waste.

The rest of the morning we go over my options, and we decide I will continue to go to the Moon River Pack on a daily basis to work as a nurse as agreed, and I shall return home to the safety of my apartment every day unless the threat from the Shadow Pack increases.

Garett is not impressed and argues every step of the way. If he has his way, he'll make me stay here so he can 'look after' me. Infuriating man.

Tori is just getting ready to leave. She has some explaining to do to her boss – she did ditch work to come and see me here, after all. Slinging her bag over her shoulder, she comes over to give me a hug.

"Oh! Before I forget, you remember McHottie? The guy who turned up at the apartment asking after you? Well, he was on the doorstep again this morning. He is getting a bit pushy. I told him you had moved out," she tells me with a wink before walking out the door, waving to Garett as she leaves.

Who the hell is this guy? Besides, how does he know where I live? I'm not sure Garett even has my home address; it's my sanctuary.

"McHottie?" Garett asks in a barely controlled voice.

"Woah, down boy. Some stranger turned up at the apartment asking after me. Seems he tried again today." I shrug this off as if it's nothing.

In reality my mind is spinning, but I have too much to think about already. Garett must sense this as he stalks towards me with a low growl, backing me to the wall again. My body reacts, arching into him as a bolt of desire fills me. I see his pupils dilate as he watches my reaction to him. Lowering his head towards mine, he stops an inch away from my lips.

"Move in with me. Let me keep you safe."

I instantly go cold, all hints of desire gone as I stiffen in his arms. Raising my eyes to meet his, I know my gaze is steely.

"Really, Garett?" I push past him, possibly a little harder than I needed to as I see him stumble a little.

I am fuming. At Garett, but mostly at myself. I should have seen this coming, but I can't help but play with fire. However, I have never been the most tactful.

"Why the hell would I move in with you? Just sit in your apartment forever and let you fight my battle for me? What is it with you males thinking I am so weak? I. Don't. Need. Protecting!" I shout at him, my anger getting the better of me.

I can see I have upset him, but I can't seem to stop myself.

"I'm just trying to help you, Ari. Why are you so stubborn? When will you learn that accepting help is not a sign of weakness? If you keep pushing, one of these days you are going to look around and there will be no one there. What the hell happened to you to make you such a bitch?" he retorts, his own pain clear to see on his face.

I flinch as if he has hit me. It might have been better if he did; bruises will heal. These types of wounds take much more time to recover from. My eyes sting, not from the harshness of his words, but from the fact they are true. I will myself not to cry as I pull on my shoes, which I had kicked off earlier, hurrying towards the door. I see my phone vibrate and flash up with a message. Grabbing it I hit out a quick text reply and shove it in my back pocket.

"Ari, I'm sorry. I didn't mean it. Please don't go."

I stop in the doorway, indecision warring through me. If I leave, then everything that he accused me of is true. But I can't stay, and I certainly can't move in with him. That just isn't an option for me, and he won't understand that.

I feel him step up behind me, close enough to touch, but not daring to. I make the decision for him and turn around, burying my face in his chest.

"I'm sorry. I know I can be a bitch. I just... It's always been just me. I've learned not to trust anyone, until I moved here and met Tori. And then before I knew it you came into my life, whether I wanted you too or not, and I've come to trust you as much as I do her. It just takes a long time to bring down walls like that," I mutter, my words muffled by his shirt, but I know he hears me as he relents, sighing as he wraps his arms around me.

"I know, Ari, I'm sorry I pushed you. I know you're not ready," he comforts me, running his hands through my hair. "Will you stay, just for a bit?" he asks, and I can hear the fear in his voice. The worry that I will walk out that door and not come back.

Leaning away I smile at him, hoping it conveys my affection towards him as I slowly shake my head. That is not a good idea. Besides, I have someone I need to meet before I head back to the pack. His smile is resigned and, as he leans forward, brushing a soft kiss across my forehead, I can see the pain in his eyes that I am causing him.

Not wanting to drag this out any further, I head towards the door, stopping briefly once I reach it to throw a saucy smile over my shoulder.

"You're still the first person I'd call if I want to get sweaty and naked," I tease, echoing the words he said to me in the bar the other night.

My comment works and he laughs, nodding at me before shooing me out of the door.

Chapter Twelve

Sitting in the busy coffee bar, I stare into my coffee, watching the steam eddy across the top of the liquid as I think over the events of the day. I feel bad about how I left things with Garett, but where he was going with his feelings and declarations was a place I was not ready to travel. Hell, I might never be ready for that. I'm too broken and damaged for someone as perfect as Garett. I'm mean, rough around the edges, and have a tendency to push people away when I don't feel safe. Garett is the opposite. Not to mention the fact that I can't seem to control my panties around Alex. Or my closeness with Seb.

I sigh. What a mess my life has become. This is why it was easier not to have any friends. The only person I had to worry about hurting was myself.

I'm so caught up in my musings that I don't notice that someone has approached me until the seat opposite me squeals as it's pulled back. With a start, I look up into the smiling face of Eric Daniels.

"You look like you've had a rough couple of days," he comments, and I smile, rolling my eyes at him.

"You really know how to compliment the ladies, Eric," I tease, chuckling as he realises his faux pas.

He looks like he is going to say something, but changes his mind. "I'm just going to get a coffee. Can I get you something?" he asks.

I shake my head and watch as he walks over to the counter to order his drink. Now I know what you're thinking. What on earth am I doing here in a coffee bar in the middle of the city meeting Dr. Hotstuff? This is exactly what I want to know. When I checked my phone earlier in the day, I found several messages from him, each one sounding more desperate, until finally he asked me to meet him here. Apparently he has something he needs to tell me. I wonder what it is, and what is so urgent that it has pulled him from work. I feel unsettled and grouchy not being able to go to work. I worked damn hard to become a nurse and now I am being stopped from doing that by supernatural bullshit. I sigh, running my hand through my hair. That's not true. I will still be able to help people, those people just happen to turn into wolves.

While Eric is standing at the coffee bar, I can't help but admire his looks. His tousled blond hair and dreamy baby blue eyes are the perfect match for his boyish good looks and beaming smile. He has the kind of face that puts you at ease with a smile, which helps with his profession, not to mention that he is a brilliant doctor. Wearing his smart blue trousers and short-sleeved white shirt, he has most of the ladies in the shop admiring him, not that he seems to notice.

I think back over our friendship. We work well together, and outside of work we have hung out a couple of times, always with Tori present. But if I'm honest, I have always pushed away any of his attempts to take our friendship further. Part of this is because he is human, but I can't keep hiding behind this excuse anymore, especially if what I suspect about him is true. He knows too much about the supernatural – he must have known a shifter, perhaps dated one. His past comments and actions over the last year are starting to make more sense now. At the hospital, when the patient came in with the carving on his back, he knew when to get me out of the room before I lost control. But the other part is because he wouldn't just be a one-night stand. I can see a future with Eric and that terrifies me. I also know that he would want more from me than a 'friends with benefits' arrangement. So, I have kept him at arm's length.

I pull myself out of my thoughts as I see Eric walking back over to our table, a coffee in one hand, and in the other a plate with an iced doughnut. Eric sits with a sweet smile, but my attention is on the doughnut. His amused chuckle drags my eyes off the doughnut, reluctantly, to his smiling face. He pushes the plate towards me.

"This is for you," he tells me, his eyebrows raising as I immediately reach forward, shoving the heavenly cake into my mouth.

I've already eaten half of it before I smile at him, pretty sure there is icing on my face.

"You shouldn't have, I'm trying to watch my figure," I joke as I inhale the rest of the doughnut. I'm licking the icing off my fingers and see that he looks nervous. "Man, it must be bad news if you're buying me doughnuts," I say in a teasing voice, trying to ease some of the tension from his shoulders.

He laughs at my comment, but doesn't relax at all. Instead, he looks even tenser. Shit. My comment must have hit a mark. What on earth is he going to tell me?

"Ari. How are you? You haven't been at work. Where are you staying at the moment?" he asks in a rush.

Woah, question overload. I raise my eyebrows at him and take a sip of my coffee as I digest his questions.

"I'm fine, I just needed some time off work. I'm staying with a friend. Anyway, how did you know I wasn't staying at the apartment?" I ask, starting to get frustrated. Since when did this become an interrogation?

"I stopped by the apartment a couple of times and knew you weren't there," he tells me, looking down into his coffee cup, distracted.

I put my coffee cup down and stare at him, not sure I'm hearing him right.

"You stopped by the apartment?" I ask. Also, what did he mean by saying he knew I wasn't there?

"Well, since that guy keeps turning up at your apartment, I wanted to check that everything was okay," he continues.

At this point I don't think that he is fully aware of what he is saying or the hole he is digging. I've never seen Eric like this. He is usually so calm and composed, but here he is, rambling and not able to meet my eyes.

"Eric, what the hell are you on about? What's going on?" I've had enough. I want answers and I want them now. I see him grimace and I feel my frustration ease. I lean forward and place my hand on his. I don't like seeing him like this. I may have been keeping my distance, but we are still friends. I think.

Eric looks at my hand on his and his face turns into a grimace once again. I'm starting to think it's me and go to pull my hand away until he grabs it with his other hand, holding mine in place.

"Ari, you're in danger."

I go still at his words, running my eyes over the man in front of me. My inner wolf comes to attention, assessing the situation for the supposed danger, and my senses go into hyperdrive. I look around the coffee bar, trying to discreetly sniff the air for any potential threat. I can't smell anything unusual. In fact, the only thing that I can really smell is Eric. Okay, I know that sounds weird, but he has always smelled interesting to me, sweet and rich like honey, different to any other scent I have smelled before.

"What do you mean I'm in danger?" I ask, keeping my tone of voice low, although it doesn't hide the slight growl that slips from me.

Eric looks at me and I'm hit with the full force of his stunning blue eyes, but even those aren't enough to distract me today.

"I've been hearing things. I have... friends. People are after you. Dangerous people. I think you should lay low for a bit," he tells me earnestly, his grip on my hand tightening a bit as he leans towards me. "I have a safe house, you could come and stay with me. I will look after you."

I pull my hand away and look at him incredulously. Is this guy serious?

"What is it with people asking me to move in with them today?" I rant, well and truly fed up. "And what do you mean you have been hearing things? Who are these friends? How do you know all this stuff?" I am practically spitting this at him as I try to keep my voice low, my anger making my words clipped and harsh.

My wolf doesn't like this. She wants me to fight or run and is pushing for control. I push her back. I can handle this; I am in control here.

"Ari, I know what you are. I know you're a werewolf."

And with that little bombshell one of the baristas comes over to the table to ask if we have everything we need, flirting to the max with Eric. Ever the gentleman, he is politely trying to get her to leave, his eyes only leaving mine for a few seconds before darting back. Normally I would find this amusing, but not today. I snap my head towards the simpering woman and narrow my eyes.

"We are fine. Thanks," I bite out.

She raises her eyebrows at me, and with another look at Eric as she leaves the table. She probably thinks I'm a jealous raging bitch but I really don't care. I have bigger fish to fry.

"Explain," I order, not in the mood for this runaround anymore.

Eric sighs, running his hand through his neat hair, messing it up in a way I've not seen before. It suits him. *Focus Ari, now is not the time.*

"I've been part of the supernatural world all my life, so I know what you are. I know you're a lone wolf and you live with a witch – who has great protection on your apartment, by the way. I've been hearing some things that worry me. Things about you. I don't know what you've done, but you have pissed off some pretty nasty people," he explains.

I lean back in my chair and think over what he is saying. Is he guarding his words because of where we are, or because he is hiding something? He may be telling the truth, that much I can tell, but he isn't telling the whole truth.

"Shadow Pack?" I ask. It has to be, but I need to know for sure.

He nods his head, his eyes worried. Dread fills my stomach. They really have come for me.

"They were my former pack, back in England," I mumble, and understanding fills his eyes.

"The patient that came in the other night, with the symbol. Was that Shadow Pack?" he asks, and I just nod. Guilt fills me that this was done to an innocent because they were sending me a message. The brutality of it is just a hint at how far they could go.

"It's not just Shadow Pack. You've also started to attract some other attention. There are some dangerous people in this city. Let me help you, Ari, please."

I rub my hand across my face, thinking through everything I have learned. Something about what Eric said is bugging me, but I can't think why. Wearily I take a sip from my coffee, hoping the caffeine will give me inspiration. He seems to know too much for a human. Even if he has been brought up by supernaturals, no one would tell a human this sort of thing, unless he was dating someone who knew this information. Unless he was a supernatural. Son of a bitch.

A deadly calm fills me. I place my coffee cup back down on the table gently, and look up at the lying, traitorous man I had started to call a friend. He can see it in my eyes and he has the decency to look nervous.

"Ari, I–"

"What are you?" I demand, not giving him the chance to finish whatever his excuse was going to be.

"Ari, I'm human, I just know–" he starts, but I cut him off again, anger practically vibrating through my body as my hands start to shake.

"Do not lie to me. What. Are. You?"

He isn't going to answer. I can see it in the way he is looking at me. Well, I am done. I push away from the table, my cup spilling in the process, covering the table in leftover coffee. I am halfway across the shop when he calls my name.

"Ari. Wait. I'm sorry, I'll tell you," he calls, his voice sounding tired and defeated.

I let him sweat it out for a moment before nodding and

walking back to my seat. I try to keep my distance. Eric has broken my trust and it will take time for him to earn it again.

"I'll listen, but you have to tell me the truth," I tell him, and my heart hurts a little at his expression. Like I have promised to give him all his hopes and dreams.

"I don't know how to do this," he admits, and I understand that. If I suddenly had to admit that I was Shadowborn, I wouldn't know how to do it either. When you have been hiding something for so long, it's difficult to break that habit. Doesn't mean I forgive him, though. I stay quiet as he is working through what he wants to say.

"There isn't really a name for what I am, but the closest thing is an Incubus," he finally tells me, not meeting my eyes, his voice barely above a whisper.

"Wait. Isn't an Incubus a sex demon?" I ask. I've never met one before. In fact, I didn't think they really existed. I've only ever heard stories about them. Suddenly I'm glad I didn't let my hormones get the better of me. He grimaces and shakes his head.

"No. Well, some are. Not me." He sighs, running his hands through his hair again. "I feed off energy, like an Incubus, but I feed off pain."

Shock fills me. He feeds off pain…

"How does that work? Where do you feed?" I ask, a sinking feeling filling my stomach. My suspicions are confirmed when he looks up at me guiltily.

"Where is the place where people feel the most pain?" he asks as disgust fills me. "I only feed a little off each person, not enough for them to feel anything but a little tired. I only feed deeper off those who are already dying."

I feel like I'm going to vomit. Anger fills me at the thought of him feeding off my patients.

"You are a doctor. You signed a Hippocratic oath to 'do no harm'. How could you?" I demand, staring at him like I've never seen him before.

It is the ultimate betrayal of trust to harm a patient. I don't care what he says about only taking a little of their energy. He has done so without gaining consent, which in my mind is assault. Those patients come to the hospital and place their trust in us to care for them. The idea that a being that can feed off of pain has been working in the hospital fills me with anger and disgust. The fact that it is Eric makes this all the harder.

"Wait, how did I not know you were anything other than human? Even Tori thought you were human," I ask, confused. Not much slips by Tori.

Eric sits silent, looking pained as I speak.

"I am very old, I can hide my presence."

I blink at him. For him to be able to do that he must be OLD, like five hundred years plus.

"Ari, I don't hurt anyone. Besides, I have to feed to live. Many of my kind like inflicting pain on humans and then feeding off it. I would *never* do that. I work as a doctor because I want to help people, not because I can feed off them. It just has the added benefit..." He trails off at my expression.

"I have to go," I say, as I pick up my bag, pushing my seat back.

"Ari, please don't go."

I stand with a sigh. Why are things never easy?

"Eric, I have somewhere I have to be. Besides I can't be around you right now. I need to think. You lied to me, but worse, you put patients in danger. I'm not sure I can forgive that," I tell him honestly.

He nods, looking resigned, almost like he expected my response.

"I understand that. Just, stay safe, okay?"

I don't answer him, just give him a slight nod before walking out of the coffee shop. I don't look back at him. I just walk to my car and begin the journey back to the pack compound.

Chapter Thirteen

park my car behind one of the main buildings at the pack compound. I place my head on the steering wheel and close my eyes. I just need a moment to myself to think through everything that I have learnt.

Eric is an Incubus. A fucking pain-eating parasite who has been feeding off my patients. I should have known. Maybe I could have done something. I sigh with frustration. What could I have done? Told my boss? I would have been thrown into the psych ward before you could say "werewolf".

My silent breakdown is interrupted by a loud bang on my car. Jerking up, I glance around for the cause of the noise. There, standing at the bonnet of my car, is a very pissed-off looking Killian. Arms crossed, he looks like he is about to burst out of his shirt if he was to flex his muscles. His scowl makes his features look harsh, especially with the scar that runs down the side of his face. He strides to the side of my car and yanks open the door.

"Glad to see you got your lazy ass back here," he spits out, glaring at me with enough hatred that I wonder what I've done to personally offend him so much. "Training room, ten minutes," he orders, before turning on his heel and striding away from me. Nope, I think he is just a dick.

I was planning to go back to the medical wing, look over the supplies and try to get my head around how things are run here, but I guess that's not going to happen now. I haul myself out of the car and walk towards where I think the training room is.

"Again!" Killian barks at me for what feels like the thousandth time that afternoon.

I growl under my breath as I pick myself off the mat where I had been thrown, brushing down my leggings in the process. *Stay calm, Ari. Patience is a virtue.* Or so I keep reminding myself. I would say I'm a pretty patient person – my job makes that a necessity. However, Killian seems to be an expert in pushing my buttons. Walking around me in a circle, with that look on his face, you would think he has just stepped in something unpleasant rather than being in the middle of training me.

First he had me running laps around the compound until I had fallen to my knees feeling like I was going to throw up, him shouting insults at me all the way round. After that he had me boxing and weight training. He has been in a foul mood all afternoon, but he seems to have cheered up a bit. Unfortunately for me, this is because we are fight training, which means he gets to throw me around.

"I've never seen a more lazy and out-of-shape wolf in all my life," he tells me, the disdain dripping from his words.

I try not to let him get me angry. At the challenge he helped me, encouraged me. Sure, he did it by insulting me, but he helped more than anyone else did. Being Alpha of another pack meant that he didn't have to follow quite the same rules as everyone else. I hoped after the fight that he would have thawed out a bit; after all, we are similar, and neither of us belong here. However, I find myself disappointed. He is treating me with as much disdain as when he first met me. Sure, he is rude to everyone, but he seems to have taken a particular dislike to me.

I face him again, dropping into the defensive stance. He has been trying to teach me basic self-defence. As it turns out I am useless in close combat, as Killian has delighted in telling me all afternoon. He walks up behind me and wraps his arms around me in a bear hug. I drop my weight and try to kick my foot back around his leg as instructed. In theory, I should be able to use his weight against him and throw him to the ground. In practice, I can't get him to go down.

"Twist your upper body more. You haven't hooked your leg properly," he scolds, his mouth close to my ear. I can feel his breath against my skin and it distracts me.

He growls and shifts his weight. He moves his hands and before I know it I am thrown across his body and land on the mats with a thud.

"Useless! Why the fuck should I bother teaching you?" he shouts at me, twisting his body so I am pinned to the floor. "Fight me! Get up!"

I struggle in my position on the floor but he is too heavy and I can't get out of his grip. I try to kick him and he pins my legs down with his own.

"Pathetic," he scolds, lowering his face towards mine. His

eyes have shifted so I am staring at his wolf. I can feel his Alpha power rising, pushing against my own. His voice has lowered when he speaks again "Pathetic," he repeats, but I am dragged under into my memories.

"Pathetic," the voice sneers at me again.

From my position where I am pinned to the floor, I can only see his face and his dark eyes piercing me with his sick gaze as it rakes over my body. His eyes are so dark they are almost black. I am too weak to fight back – months of being locked in the dark and being underfed will do that to you.

"Do as we say and we will let you rejoin the pack. You will get regular meals again. You can see the sun. And once you have proved your loyalty to Shadow Pack, we will start training you again."

I am still being punished from when I tried to escape nearly six months ago. Since then I have been locked in the dark cell they call my room and only given enough food to keep me alive. The only time I have been permitted to leave is to see the Alpha, like now. All these meetings go the same, dragged before the Alpha and the Elders, ordered to use my Shadowborn powers at their discretion. I refuse, get punished and dragged back to my 'room'. If I'm particularly unlucky, I will get brought to the Alpha alone. Without the Elders to hold him back, the punishments are always significantly worse.

Today is like the other days: the Alpha is stalking around the back of the room, watching as his young Beta, Terrance, pushes me around and 'teaches me my place'. I look up at Terrance and spit at him.

"Fuck. You," *is the only response I give them.*

My head snaps to one side as I am backhanded for my comment. Terrance's hands move from my shoulders to my neck. My heart kicks into overdrive as my airway begins to be cut off. I know he won't kill me – they need me – but that doesn't stop the panic as I can't catch my breath.

"Terrance," *the Alpha calls. Immediately the pressure from my throat is removed and I can breathe again. I lay on the floor, gasping, as Terrance walks back towards the Alpha.* "Ariana, I have a different proposition for you."

I know I am in trouble as he has used my name. Usually I am just 'the Shadowborn' or 'Girl'. I prop myself up on one elbow and look towards the Alpha and the Elders.

"Terrance has offered to Mate with you. Now that you are nearly eighteen, you need to be Mated. We can't have a female running around unmated. You will be given space and a small measure of freedom, food, and we will even begin your training again. I am sure that under Terrance's... guidance, you will become a valuable member of our pack."

I feel the blood draining from my face as he speaks. I think my life is bad now, but under Terrance's 'guidance' it would be ten times worse. Guidance my ass. I would be under his control and that's what they want. At the moment he can't be alone in a room with me, because of what I am and pack rules. As soon as we are Mated, there will be nothing to stop him from doing whatever he wanted. What I don't understand is why they are asking.

"Never," *I rasp out, my throat raw after the abuse it's just been put through.*

The Alpha's expression never changes, but I can see by the way his body stills that I have pissed him off. Terrance looks like he wants to strangle me again. The Alpha nods at him, and with a sick smile he walks up to me, kicking my arm out from underneath me. I fall to the ground with a cry and he straddles me again, pushing me into the ground, his hands circling my neck. He leans down so his mouth is next to my ear.

"There is only one way out of this, Ariana. You will be mine," he whispers, his breath hot against my tender skin.

I realise now why they told me. They weren't asking. The Alpha was warning me that things could get much worse if I didn't do as they said.

Hands tighten around my neck again and I gasp for breath, my vision starting to dim around the edges. A small part of me hopes that Terrance will take it too far, that he will kill me in his anger.

"Pathetic."

"Ari!"

I can hear my name being shouted. Why are they so loud? My head is pounding.

"Ariana, snap out of it!" The angry voice continues, but I'm sure I hear a tinge of worry.

"What did you do to her?" a familiar voice shouts, although I'm not used to hearing him sound so mad. What's his name again? A gentle hand touches my arm and a warm vanilla scent surrounds me. Seb. I feel my body relax a little. He won't let me get hurt.

"We were practising some self defence moves and she just went stiff in my arms. I let her go and she went limp, staring at the ceiling. She then her eyes closed and she started shaking, like she was scared. She kept whispering a name. It was like someone was hurting her," the voice continues. Killian, I realise, although I've not heard his voice so soft before. Sounds like he actually cares. Ha!

"She gets flashbacks. Something must have triggered her," Seb mutters as he gently lifts my upper body into his lap.

I open my eyes slightly and see a worried Seb looking down at me. A cute smile crosses his face as he sees me awake.

"Hey, beautiful," he says, which makes me smile.

I'm aware of movement down by my feet and I glance down to see Killian staring at me, his eyes glowing as he fights his wolf.

"Flashbacks. Like memories. You mean this happened–" He cuts himself off, a growl reverberating through his chest. He holds his arms open and gestures for Seb to pass me across to him.

Seb looks down at me and then back to the angry Alpha.

"Give her to me," Killian growls and I can feel the power in his words, but I can hear an undercurrent of something that sounds like concern in his voice. I must be hearing things.

I can feel Seb try to fight against the order, but there is no use. Even I would struggle to fight an order from someone as powerful as Killian.

I am passed over to Killian where he cradles me in his arms. We stay this way until Alex comes storming into the gym. Killian's face is set in a stormy scowl as he holds me, like he was being forced, but the whole time I have been clutched to his chest as he slowly strokes my back, trying to calm my frantic breathing. I even tried to get up once, and was growled at so fiercely that I decided to stay where I was. I'm not even sure I would have been able to break out of his grip.

"Killian, I'm okay now. You can let me up," I tell him.

He just growls at me half-heartedly and tightens his grip.

"Bloody Alpha-male babies," I mutter under my breath, and smirk as he hears me and bares his teeth at me.

To be honest, although I bitch and moan, I feel safe in his arms. His Alpha power calls to mine and calms me. If we didn't drive each other crazy, we would probably make a good match. Maybe in a different world, that would work.

"What happened?" Alex demands. I can hear anger and frustration in his tone. I'm not surprised. I have been nothing but trouble since I got here.

"She had a flashback and now Mr. Macho Alpha over here won't let her go," Seb fills Alex in, not worried about the backlash from Killian now that Alex is here.

Killian growls at both of the men as they try to get closer, sounding more wolf than man. His stance changes as he tries to put himself between me and Alex, while still keeping me in his lap. I glance up at him and see his eyes have turned fully wolf. What the hell is going on?

"Killian, let go of Ari, I'm here now," Alex comments and he comes closer.

What is it with these guys wanting to hold me? I am perfectly capable of getting up and walking. It's embarrassing enough having a flashback without it setting off their protective instincts.

Werewolves are naturally very protective of their pack and those they consider family, but I've literally just walked in their pack. Besides, Killian isn't part of this pack either, so I don't understand where his protective behaviour is coming from. Seb seems to be behaving himself, but as one of the 'lower' pack members those instincts won't be as strong. His feelings towards me are his own, not some wolfy bullshit. The stronger the wolf, the stronger the instincts.

Killian growls louder at Alex, so fiercely that it causes the Beta to stop in his tracks. He looks across at Seb, who also looks pale at this point. I thought it was from all this Alpha power floating around in the air, but with the looks they are giving each other I am not so sure anymore.

"Mine," says a guttural voice from above me as arms tighten around me.

"Um, excuse me?" I retort, looking up at the Alpha.

I hear Alex curse under his breath as he crouches down to our level like he is trying to tame a wolf cub during their first shift. What the hell does he mean by 'mine'?

"Seb, go and get Alpha Mortlock. And Isa, we might need their help," he instructs, not taking his eyes off Killian, as if he is afraid what he might do if his back was turned. "Ari, just stay still. I know that this will be difficult, but try keep your mouth shut."

I'm just about to protest when the angry werewolf holding me snarls again. Alex spreads out his arms wide in a placating gesture.

"Killian, I'm not going to hurt her, but you need to put Ari down."

I hear running footsteps and glance around to see Alpha Mortlock hurrying over, his eyes widening at what he is seeing.

"What happened?" he demands of Alex, who stands up and walks over to the Alpha.

With their voices low, I can't hear much of what they are

saying, only snippets. Seb is looking at me worriedly, but smiles at me when he sees me looking at him.

"… Have they Mated?" I hear Mortlock ask, which has me jerking in Killian's arms.

Fuck this.

"Mated?" I shout, ignoring the growl coming from Killian.

I jump up out of his hold, even though he tightens his hold on my arms to keep me close. That's going to bruise. Right now, all I care about is getting out of his arms. Killian comes towards me, like he is going to grab me again, so I drop into a defensive position.

"Mine," he growls again.

I've had enough. I jump forward and punch him in the face, hard enough to make him take a step back. Stunned, he stares at me for a moment until I see his eyes start to turn back to normal. Hand on his jaw, he narrows his eyes at me before glaring at Alpha Mortlock and storming out of the room.

I spin around to look at the stunned males behind me.

"Will someone please explain what the fuck just happened?"

Chapter Fourteen

We are back in the family room of the main building. Alpha Mortlock and Lena sit on one of the leather sofas, the latter wringing her hands as she watches me pace up and down the room. Alex is in his usual place to the Alpha's right, propping up the wall, arms crossed and a scowl across his features.

Isa walks into the room and heads straight towards me. With a hand on my shoulder, she takes me to the side, lowering her voice as she looks at me seriously.

"I hear you have problems with a man," she tells me in her thick German accent. "Would you like me to pummel him?" she asks sincerely.

I raise my eyebrows at her, struggling not to laugh at the Gamma offering to beat up Killian. Now that is a fight I would pay to see. A warm feeling fills my chest, and I realise with a shock that it's the feeling of belonging. I look at the woman in front of me in bemusement. When did she start considering me as someone she would protect? Because that is exactly what she is offering by threatening to beat up Killian.

"Is Killian not part of the pack? Does he not get protection?" I ask. Surely she is not being serious.

With a wink, she chuckles softly.

"Men who think women cannot look after themselves deserve being shown otherwise," she tells me conspiringly.

I let out a stunned laugh. I like this woman.

"I'll keep that in mind, Isa. Thank you," I reply, and I hope that she knows from my tone how much her comments mean to me.

Isa nods her head in acknowledgement and goes to take her spot behind the Alpha. I begin pacing up and down the room again before Seb walks in and wraps his arms around me. I go still at the sudden contact, but as soon as I smell his sweet scent and know it's him, I relax in his arms. I'm glad he is here. I would have insisted, had the Alpha not invited him. I'm not sure when it happened, but Seb is part of my little family now.

"Ariana, please take a seat. We have a lot to discuss," Alpha Mortlock says, bringing my attention back to the room.

I give Seb a grateful smile and squeeze his arm affectionately as I pull out of his arms. I walk towards the other leather sofa and sit down so I am facing the Alpha and Lena. I had expected Seb to sit next to me but I can't see him. I spin in my seat and see him standing by the door. I raise my eyebrows at him and gesture to the seat next to me. He widens his eyes at me and looks over to Alpha Mortlock, like he is asking for permission. Mortlock nods and Seb comes and sits next to me with a smile. I struggle not to sigh at this show of pack politics. Just because Seb is not as strong as the others in the room does not mean that he should be standing on the sidelines. Sure, Mortlock is much more lenient than other Alphas, from my limited experience, but this still frustrates me.

Mortlock looks around the room and clears his throat.

"Now we are all here, we can get started," he announces. Guess that means Killian isn't part of this discussion.

I haven't seen him since he skulked off after the showdown

in the gym. What the hell was all that about anyway? Anger, frustration and a little bit of fear are all running through me and I have to take a deep breath to calm myself.

"Ariana, how much do you know about Mated pairs?" Alpha Mortlock asks me.

I feel the blood drain from my face and can feel all eyes in the room on me. I stand up, my fight-or-flight instinct kicking in. This cannot be happening. Especially not with an asshole like Killian. I am planning my escape from this room for the second time in less than a week when someone takes my hand. I look down and see that it's Seb.

"Ari." A voice calls my name and I look across the room to see Alex is walking towards me. "It's alright, let's work this out together." His voice is soft and rings with honesty. He has never spoken to me like this before.

I turn and focus on Seb's face. There is nothing there but worry for me. He nods at me and gently pulls at my hand to get me to sit again. I slowly sit back down, fighting my natural response to bail on situations like this.

"Mating is for life," I answer Mortlock's question. I don't know much, but I do know this.

The Alpha nods his head in acknowledgement of my response, and my unspoken fact that I know next to nothing about the intricacies of pack life.

"Any shifters can choose to form a Mating bond, but as you said, these are permanent and for life. These should not be rushed and we don't see these often, as most shifters tend to use the human form of bonding and commit to marriage instead."

I nod to show my understanding, not quite sure how this relates to me.

"True Mated pairs are a different ball game altogether. We don't see these often anymore, but a true Mated pair is when two shifters are drawn to each other and are destined to be together. They are your perfect partner." Mortlock stops at this point and smiles at Lena, takes her hand and places a kiss on the back of it. I can see the love the two of them share from here.

"The bond, once accepted, is also for life," he continues.

I latch onto this piece of information. I have a bad feeling about where this conversation is going.

"So the pair bond is not inevitable? You don't have to accept?" I ask, a note of desperation in my voice.

Mortlock sighs and looks back at me, shaking his head. "No, the bond has to be accepted by both shifters. It doesn't happen often, but there are records of rejected bonds. But once the bond has been triggered, it is very difficult to resist. If the bond is accepted, the shifters will have access to each other's power," he finishes telling me.

"Okay, so why are we having this conversation?" I ask a little bluntly. I know it's rude to talk to the Alpha that way, but my nerves are making me feisty.

Mortlock pauses, looking like he really doesn't want to be having this conversation.

"Killian is showing signs that you might be his true Mate." I go still as he continues. "The overprotective behaviour, not letting another male close. It's all behaviour ingrained in us to make sure another male doesn't mate with our true Mate. When the bond has been accepted, this will calm down. It never goes away, but it gets easier." He smiles at me in a way that says he understands. I'm sure he does, but I don't like that he keeps saying 'when', like I'm going to accept the bond.

"But I don't feel anything!" I practically shout. Surely if we were a Mated pair I should be feeling this 'bond' as well.

Mortlock shoots me a look like he doesn't believe me. "You

don't feel drawn to him in any way? Your powers don't call to each other? Even if this was true, the bond often takes time to grow. Killian's was set off at the thought of others hurting you."

I run my hands through my hair, trying to take in the overload of information.

"So why isn't Killian here? Why is it just me having the lesson?" I ask. Where was that bastard anyway?

Mortlock sighs and looks at Lena as if for strength.

"Killian is having a difficult time accepting all of this." I am about to protest at this comment when he continues. "He had a mate before. Julie. They loved each other and decided to take the Mating bond. He was Alpha of another pack." Alpha Mortlock pauses and runs his hand over his face. "He made a bad decision and there was an attack on his pack. Everyone died, including Julie, and the bond was broken. I have never experienced that, but I am told it's like a piece of your body is ripped open and the wound never heals. For him to now find he has a pair bond... well, I can't imagine all the thoughts running through his head right now. Just give him time." His voice is rough as he talks.

A lot more of his behaviour makes sense now, and I definitely understand his attitude. I can't imagine the pain of losing someone that you are bonded to. Even my shrivelled, broken heart can understand the heartbreak of losing someone like that. If I lost Tori, Garett, or even Seb, I think I would break.

"So what happens next?" I ask, a little subdued from the turn of conversation.

Alpha Mortlock shrugs and a slight smile graces his lips.

"That is up to you, like I said. You don't *have* to accept the bond. I would suggest that you don't rush anything, either way."

I nod at his sage advice. It may be my first instinct to push the idea of a bond away and flee immediately, but perhaps it's time to stop running. I'm still not accepting the bond, but I'm starting to feel like I might be a part of something here in the pack, and I find I'm reluctant to leave it before I've even properly started.

"So when can I start in the medical wing? I'm starting to feel twitchy not being at work," I say with a small smile.

I had expected the Alpha to smile, but instead he looks weary, rubbing a hand over his face. Lena leans across and takes his hand, stroking it to comfort the Alpha. The image makes me smile, the large Alpha receiving comfort from his small female mate. Equals.

"I was hoping you could start immediately. I was coming to find you when Seb came to get me. One of the pups is very unwell. She developed a fever and we thought it would pass but she has taken a turn for the worse," Mortlock explains.

I jump to my feet, the need to see this child increasing as he speaks. I feel guilty that I have kept a child waiting that needs my help because of my freak-out at Killian.

"What are we waiting for? Let's go."

I brush hair from the little girl's forehead. She has a fever of 39C, or 102.2 Fahrenheit as it is here – I still can't get used to that. I look down at the sick child. Lottie, her parents told me her name was. She is a little younger than Jessica, only six years old. Her mother hasn't left her side since I arrived, holding her hand and talking to her the whole time. It's dark outside now, but I'm not sure what the time is. I have learnt a lot about Lottie in that time. She likes to climb trees and wrestle with the other children. She often gets into trouble for getting into fights when sticking up for the smaller wolves. She is going to be strong when she grows up.

Alpha Mortlock took me straight to her after a quick trip to the medical building for some supplies. Seb has been running things back and forth to the medical building for me, as she is too unwell to move and a human hospital is not the place for her. When the Alpha came to check on how things were going, I pulled him aside and told him he needed to get a doctor here. I can't be here 24-7 and if someone else becomes unwell, I would struggle to spread myself between my patients. I also need a doctor, as nurses can't give medications that aren't prescribed, and I don't want to lose my licence. In an emergency I can give fluids, which is what I did. The Alpha reluctantly agreed with me and managed to borrow a doctor from a local pack who came over and prescribed some IV antibiotics. Lottie's mother broke down at seeing her little girl hooked up to machines, but I explained that she had a severe infection and this would hopefully allow her to heal quicker.

The doctor left a couple of hours ago and Lottie's condition has stabilised enough that we can move her to the medical building. Her temperature has lowered now and she has even woken up enough to complain that she is hungry. A nurse from another pack attended with the doctor and agreed to stay the night to keep an eye on the little girl.

I hear the door open and look over my shoulder to see Alex. I look across to the other nurse, who nods at me, letting me know she has got this. I leave the little girl's side and walk over to Alex.

"How is she?" he asks quietly, glancing over at Lottie.

The pack is struggling with one of their pups being so unwell, being fiercely protective of their young.

"She has stabilised now. She will be running around causing havoc again before you know it," I tell him with a tired smile.

"When was the last time you took a break?" Alex asks with a frown.

I shrug. I've lost track of the hours. I yawn as I pull my phone from my back pocket, surprised to see it's 10 o'clock in the evening. I see a message from Tori telling me she had seen my message that I am not going home tonight. When I saw how poorly Lottie was, I decided it would be best for me to stay onsite. It's been a LONG day. Alex gently puts his hand on my arm and starts to pull me towards the door.

"Come on, come with me," he instructs softly. I look over my shoulder at the little girl and her mum, not wanting to leave them. "Nurse Beth has everything under control. Besides, there is a rota to keep an eye on things. One of us will be here constantly."

I frown at him. "You didn't do that when I was looking after her," I comment.

"While we trust the Alpha's word that Nurse Beth can be trusted, we take looking after our young very seriously and aren't going to risk that. We trust you," he says simply. That warm feeling in my heart fills again and I have to look away from the expression in his eyes, not quite ready to acknowledge what I can see in them. I glance over at Lottie again, and Beth smiles at me.

"Don't worry Ari, I'll watch her," she assures me, and I can hear the sincerity in her words.

I smile at her and cast one last look over towards Lottie before turning back around to follow Alex.

"Ari, wait!" a voice calls me.

I turn to see Lottie's mother, Mary, just before she wraps her arms around me, hugging me tightly. I startle slightly at the sudden contact, but relax and hug her in return. We don't say anything – we don't need to; her gratitude shines through her eyes. She squeezes my hand before going back to her daughter's side.

I look back at Alex, who is smiling at me. "What?" I ask him, raising an eyebrow in question.

"Nothing. Come on," he tells me, taking my hand in his as he leads me out of the room.

I am so shocked that he is holding my hand that I don't think to ask where we are going. I debate pulling my hand away, but it feels quite nice. I pull a face at that thought. Since when have I gone from groaning when I see Alex to liking the feel of his hand in mine? I pull my hand away from his. Spending all this time with the pack is making me soft. I expect Alex to say something about the space now between us, but instead he smiles at me with a look of understanding. It's unnerving.

"Where are we going, anyway?" I ask, as I see we are walking towards the woods.

He grins and this worries me. No good can come from a smile like that.

"We are going for a run. It's time to shift."

Chapter Fifteen

I'm leaning against a tree with my arms crossed, pretending that the sight of Alex shirtless in front of me isn't affecting me at all. My wolf, on the other hand, has no qualms about letting him know she likes what she sees, pushing against me for control.

"Remind me again why we are doing this?" I ask him, trying, and failing, to keep my eyes on his face.

"Because you need to learn to shift properly so you can control your wolf better. She is constantly pushing for control because you suppress her. She is you. Besides, we will be having a pack run soon, and you will be expected to take part. I thought you could use the practice." I am about to argue with this and he raises his eyebrows. "Watching you shift at the social was painful. Do you really want to go through that process again?" he asks.

Fine. He isn't wrong. Besides, the thought of having to shift in front of the whole pack, again, makes my blood run cold. Maybe I do need the practice. Wait, what does he mean watching me shift was painful? I didn't see him there at the challenge and everyone turned their backs. Sneaky bastard.

Sighing, I move away from the tree and start removing my clothes, turning slightly so I'm not facing Alex full on. Out the corner of my eye, I can see Alex doing the same.

"So why isn't Seb or someone doing this with me?" I ask. I still don't feel fully comfortable around Alex yet, although he is growing on me. *Like mould.*

"Your wolf is so suppressed, I wasn't sure if Seb could handle you if you turned on him. I didn't think you would want to risk that," he tells me, and I agree with him.

I would never forgive myself if I hurt Seb. Not that I ever would, but Alex is right: I can't always control my wolf, especially once I've shifted. I hadn't thought about the possibility that I could hurt Seb. In my old pack, I was only ever surrounded by powerful wolves, as they never risked putting me with the weaker wolves in case I escaped.

I push down my jeans and underwear, bending slightly to take my feet out of the legs. I can feel Alex's hot gaze on me and it does things to me that I would rather not acknowledge. I straighten up and look him in the eyes, so I see the moment when he can sense my arousal by the way his eyes flash, his wolf making his feelings clear.

"Are we doing this or what?" I ask, trying to ignore the predatory look on his face.

I can see him struggling to take his eyes off me as he nods.

"Okay–" He stops to clear his throat, which makes me smirk. "Okay, shift, show me how you do it," he orders.

I roll my eyes at the order and kneel on the floor. I close my eyes and go to the place where my wolf resides inside me. I coax her forward and she rushes to take control. The shift hits me hard, making me fall to all fours. I grunt at the effort of it, my body screaming out as the shift takes over my body. I am aware of Alex moving to my side, kneeling next to me.

"You're fighting her, like she is a separate part of you. Welcome her: you are one," he tells me softly, encouraging the change.

I try to focus on his words, and after what feels like a lifetime the pain ends and I open my eyes again.

I raise my muzzle and look around me, jumping back in shock that a human man is crouched next to me. I jump into a defensive position, baring my fangs in warning. He puts his hands out to the side. I don't think he means me harm.

"Easy, Ari. I'm not going to hurt you. You know me," the human tells me.

Ari is the human who shares my body and I can tell something is different. She has given me more control this time. Usually she is controlling my actions and even my thoughts. It is exhausting. I sniff the air and I realise the human is right; I do recognise his scent. Alex. I sit on my hindquarters and watch him, my head tilted.

"Alright, alright." He laughs at me before getting onto hand and knees.

Closing his eyes I watch as he changes to a large black wolf, with white dabbling up his front legs and the tips of his ears. He makes it look effortless. I hope human Ari is paying attention. That is what we could have if she stopped fighting me. Wolf-Alex turns his big head to look at me and a playful look enters his gaze. Giving me a wolfy grin, he shifts his weight and I

know he is going to pounce on me. I shift into a defensive position before darting to the side of him just as he leaps towards
me. I race off deeper into the woods, aware of him on my tail.

This goes on for a couple of hours, chasing each other and
playing. This is nice. Other than shifting with Bear-Garett, we
have never played in this form before. Our pack was cruel,
especially in this form. I stop for a drink at a small stream,
drinking my fill after running around. Wolf-Alex is doing the
same next to me. All of a sudden, he jumps me from the side,
play-biting at my ears. I growl, but softly so he knows I am
playing. He has me pinned to the ground and I can see when
something changes in his eyes. Human-Ari and I are so shocked
by what we see that Human-Ari gains the upper hand and
shifts.

The shift back to human is quick and I find myself still
pinned under Alex's wolf. He winks at me in a very un-wolflike
manner before shifting back to his human form. I groan as his
full weight falls on me and am about to complain until I see his
look of arousal, which has me stilling. So I can see what he is
doing, he moves towards me slowly, lowering his lips until they
are an inch from mine. I blame the adrenaline from the shift for
what happens next.

I surge forward from my position on the ground and crush my lips to his. With a masculine groan he returns my kisses, rough and urgent, like he has wanted to do this for a long time. My hands go up to his head, twisting into his shoulder-length hair. His hands roam along my body and I can feel his arousal pressed against my leg. I hear a howl in the distance and I am startled away from him. I push him away, our breathing heavy as we try to untangle our limbs. I climb up from the ground, looking anywhere but at the evidence of his arousal and start searching for where we left our clothes.

"Are we going to talk about this?" Alex asks from the ground, propped up on one arm. His voice sounds resigned, like he already knows my answer.

"Nothing to talk about," I tell him, forcing my voice to sound cheery.

I thank the gods when I find my clothes, hurrying into them. I throw Alex's towards him.

"Put some pants on. You're distracting," I tell him, trying to make my tone teasing.

I hear him sigh before the telltale sound of someone getting changed reaches my ears. I make sure I am facing in the opposite direction, not sure if I could stop myself from touching him if I see him naked again.

"Bye then. Thanks!" I call out before I hurry off towards the medical building.

I don't sleep well that night. My thoughts are running riot through my head, along with worry for Lottie. I stopped by the room she was staying in to check on her and found her and her mother fast asleep. Nurse Beth informed me her temperature has dropped further and she is responding well to treatment.

I kissed Garett *and* Alex today, not to mention Killian showing signs of having a true Pair bond with me. And there was Seb… Now, this was why packs were messy. I don't want a relationship with *anyone*. Besides, Alex was probably just feeling high off our run and the kiss didn't mean anything. Killian certainly doesn't want anything to do with me. He couldn't get away from me fast enough once he had snapped out of his protective daze.

I look in the mirror in the borrowed bedroom that I am staying in, and sigh at the grey circles under my eyes, proof of my restless night. I brush an invisible piece of lint off my white shirt and black jeans, pulling my hair up into a loose bun. I am planning on spending the morning in the medical room, so I need to be dressed sensibly. It's strange not wearing scrubs.

Walking downstairs, I head to the treatment room where Lottie is staying. I am greeted by an animated little girl talking a hundred words-per-minute. Lottie's mother comes over to me with a beaming smile on her face.

"She is so much better, thank you!" she says, her eyes moist with unshed tears.

I smile, pleased to see Lottie has responded so well to treatment. I take her vitals and am happy to see they are all normal. I turn back to Mary.

"She can probably go back to your cabin today, but she will still need antibiotics. One more via IV, which I will give now, and the rest can be taken orally." I turn to look at Lottie and put my stern face on. "But you can only go if you promise to rest up for a few days, deal?" I ask, knowing what her reaction would be.

She frowns as she thinks over her options before she nods and gives me a bit of a smile.

"Okay, I promise!" she replies happily.

I go to prepare the last dose of IV antibiotics and get a handover from Nurse Beth. She is going back to her pack tonight, so I want to know any details that might be important once she has gone.

Two hours later and I am cleaning down the treatment room now that Lottie has gone home. I was given a list of home visits that will need to be done at some point either today or tomorrow. Mostly older wolves or the younger children, just to check in on them. I have one pregnant wolf to visit as well. I am just getting a bag of equipment ready to go out on my visits when I hear the door open again.

"One second!" I call out, as I finish wiping down the desk.

I look up and am surprised to see Garett standing in the doorway, an odd look on his face.

"Garett!" I call out, ridiculously happy to see him.

I walk straight up to him and take him by surprise by wrapping my arms around him. He lets out a surprised grunt and wraps his arms around me in return.

"How come you're here?" I ask, pulling back from his chest to look up at his face.

"Tori told me that you were staying here last night and I wanted to check you were okay. I bumped into Sebastian, though, he told me about Killian. Were you going to tell me about him?" Garett asks, his voice getting louder as his frustration rises.

I sigh and gesture for him to follow me, walking out of the treatment room and upstairs to the room I have been staying in. I let him walk in before I do, and shut the door behind me.

"So that's it then? You bonded with him? Your 'True Mate.'" He practically spits these last words at me, his body shaking with rage.

He strides forward and wraps his arms around me. I am confused at his change of attitude until I hear him inhale and I realise he isn't hugging me.

"Did you just sniff me?" I shout, pushing him away from me. "Do you even know me, Garett? Of course I haven't bonded with him. In fact, I nearly knocked him out when he tried that macho Alpha bullshit on me!"

I'm fuming and pace up and down the room, trying to cool my temper. I can't believe that Garett thinks that I would just accept a mating bond with someone at the snap of their fingers. Or that he would sniff me to see if my scent has changed through bonding, or through sex. Was my word not good enough?

"Why does this even matter to you?" I shout back at him, my anger at him for not trusting my word makes my words harsh.

"Because I love you!" he roars.

I stare at him, frozen in place at his admission. My mouth drops open but I have no idea how to respond.

"Wh– I... Huh?" I stammer, and I can see the moment he calms himself down.

He knows I have a tendency to run after dramatic declarations or when I can't deal with my emotions.

"Ari, wait," he says, hurrying towards me even though I haven't moved.

I don't think anyone has ever loved me before. The love that Tori and I have for each other is different, and even that took me a while to understand. But a love like what Garett is proposing is something I never thought I would get to experience.

He backs me up against the wall and places his hand gently on my cheek.

"Ever since I saw you, when you first came into my bar, I knew. You were so tiny and you had this hollow look in your eyes like you couldn't trust anyone, but when you were around Tori you smiled and I knew I was doomed. I tried to tell myself you needed a friend, and as you grew into the person you are now I could see the fire in you, the passion to do good and not to let your past hold you back." I find myself watching his lips as he speaks.

No one has ever said things like this to me, and I know he is telling the truth. I can feel him watching me and I flick my eyes up to him. He looks hungry.

"Fuck it," he says under his breath, and leans forward to press his lips to mine.

As his lips press gently into mine it's like a dam breaks and I push forward, deepening the kiss as I wrap my arms around him. His lips match my greedy kisses, pressing me back into the wall, reminding me of our kiss yesterday. His mouth leaves mine and kisses a trail along my jaw and down my neck, his hands roaming up to my breasts, his fingers gently tweaking my nipples. I moan and press myself against him, gasping as I feel his cock straining against his trousers. I slide my hand down inside the front of his tight jeans and grab onto his cock, his breath coming out half-gasp, half-groan. I run my hand up and down, and enjoy the feel of the contrast between the velvety softness of the skin to the solid hardness of his arousal, espe-cially as he calls out my name like a prayer. I thread my other hand through his hair and pull his head back from where he is still kissing my neck. His neck arches and I can see he is getting off on the pain from me pulling his hair – kinky. With an evil smile I pull his lips to mine, enjoying the feeling of his cock twitching in my other hand.

"Bed. Now," I order, my wolf adding our power to the command in agreement.

I feel a brief shock of surprise at her agreeing, Garett is a bear shifter, after all, and while it still happens, interbreeding is frowned upon. I push these thoughts away as Garett lifts me up. Wrapping my legs around his waist he carries me over to the bed. With me in this position my intimate parts are pressed up against his cock and I wiggle my hips as he walks, savouring the masculine groan that passes his lips. He drops me down and I pull myself up the bed.

Pulling his shirt over his head Garett drops it to the floor and pins me in place with his eyes. Climbing onto the bed, he crawls towards me, a slight predatory growl emitting from deep in his chest. I admire his thick muscles and they way they bunch up as he moves. I run my hands over him as he reaches me, only for him to pin me down to the bed. I wrap my legs around his waist and twist us so I am on top. His eyes burn with desire as I straddle him, moving my hips as I feel him straining against his trousers.

"Too many clothes," he comments, his voice deep with passion.

I give him a wink and crawl off him, standing to remove my jeans and underwear. I turn away from him as I do this so he gets a view of my ass as I bend over. I turn back towards him and see that he is now naked, his clothes in a forgotten pile on the floor. His cock sitting proudly, his hand wrapped around it as he strokes it leisurely, an adoring look on his face. I stalk back towards him, slowly unbuttoning my shirt as I go. I reach up behind the shirt and remove my strapless bra, leaving the shirt in place, unbuttoned. Looking like a man starved, he reaches towards me, pulling me on top of him. Laughing, I push up onto my hands so I can look down at him. His pupils have dilated and I can see his bear is close to the surface. He leans forward and kisses down my collar bone until he gets to my breasts, taking one of my nipples in his mouth, while his other hand comes up to tweak the other. I throw my head back, a satisfied sigh leaving my lips. Desire shoots down straight to my core. I straddle him again, his cock pressing against my inner thigh. His free hand strokes down my side and over my hip. When he finally reaches where I want him I let out a moan, his thumb flicking over my clit in lazy circles. I run my hands over his strong shoulders and back, my nails dragging across his skin as his fingers slip inside me. I cry out as they fill me, my nails digging deeper into his skin as they start to pick up rhythm. I hear his breath catch as I move one of my hands to his cock, slowly pumping it with my hand. I rub my thumb over the top of him, enjoying the way his breath hisses out from behind clenched teeth.

"Ari," he warns me.

I rise up onto my knees and guide him to my entrance. I cry out as I sink down onto his cock, savouring the slight burn that comes from being filled completely. I hear him curse under his breath as one hand comes to my hip and the other cups my cheek as he watches me. I start to rock my hips, my hands gripping onto his shoulders as I move. Moving his hand from my cheek to my clit he starts circling it again and I lose myself in the rhythm of our movements, all of which are controlled by me.

I tend not to sleep with more powerful shifters as they are dominating, whereas I can take more control with weaker shifters. With Garett I don't feel I have to fight to be in control. He is just interested in making sure I receive pleasure – which means that I get to set the pace.

I look at his face again and the look of pure desire has me crying out as my orgasm hits me. I feel myself clenching around him as he finds his own release. The feel of him coming inside me is almost enough to make me orgasm again. He pulls me towards him and kisses me, gently this time, as he runs his hands over my arms and back.

I climb off him, groaning slightly as he pulls out of my body. Sex is messy. They always leave that bit out in the romance books. I go to leave, but Garett pulls me back on the bed. I laugh as he climbs over me, kissing me in a way that makes me want to pin him to the bed and demand he fuck me again. But with a sigh I roll out from underneath him, I have work to do. I stand up and throw a wink at Garett before scooping up my discarded underwear and heading to the bathroom, the ache between my thighs the telltale sign of good sex. I pull the door closed behind me to clean myself off.

Once I'm done, I pull my underwear back on and do up my bra, deciding to leave the shirt unbuttoned. I open up the bathroom door when there is a loud slam. I spin to the source of the noise and see Killian in the doorway, a look of pure rage on his face as he takes in the scene before him. Looking like he is going to shed his skin and turn into his wolf, he takes a menacing step towards Garett, who has jumped off the bed and dropped into a fighting stance.

In a voice more wolf than human, Killian spits out at Garett, "What the fuck have you done to my Mate?"

Anger instantly fills me, killing my buzz. Oh, for fuck's sake.

Chapter Sixteen

"Killian, what the fuck do you think you are doing?" I shout, completely pissed off and mortified that he has barged in on us.

At the sound of my voice his head whips around to look at me, and then he seems to calm a little. He takes a step towards me and I get a good look at him for the first time since yesterday. His eyes are wide and glowing, fully consumed by his wolf. His chest is panting like he has run here and, from the state of his clothing, I think he has. He has bits of branch and undergrowth caught in his clothing like he has been hiding out in the woods, which for all I knew, he has been. Now that he has seen me, I can see the moment he gives into his instincts and starts stalking towards me.

"Killian, stop," I order, my power filling the room with my frustration.

I shift my weight and my open shirt moves, grabbing his attention. His eyes narrow on my exposed skin, halting his movements. All of a sudden I can feel his power rushing to meet me as he darts forward, and pushes me up against the wall and buries his nose into the crook of my neck, growling as he does so.

"I can smell him on you." I can feel the vibrations of his

growling voice through my body from where he is pressed up against me. A sick part of me is turned on by his behaviour.

The other part is just pissed off. I shove my hands against his chest to push him away. To my dismay, he only moves back a couple of inches and looks like he is going to come closer again.

"Keep your hands off her," Garett's deep voice fills the room as he comes closer, his eyes flitting from me to Killian.

I appreciate Garett hanging back, allowing me to deal with this. He knows full well that I can hold my own, and that I don't deal well with controlling behaviour. He also knows that I will kick his ass if he comes swooping in to the rescue like a knight in fucking shining armour when I am perfectly capable of whooping Killian's butt. Killian on the other hand, has a different idea.

His head turns sharply to stare at Garett, his teeth fully exposed in a snarl and I can see the tips of his canines have lengthened into fangs. Dropping into a fighting stance, he charges at Garett, leaping towards him at the last second and shifting into wolf mid-air. The sound of ripping clothes and snarling animals fills the room as Garett shifts to protect himself.

Normally I would say that a large bear shifter would beat a lone wolf shifter in most fights. However, Killian is huge. I have never seen a wolf so big before. The snow-white tips of his ears almost reach my shoulders. I briefly admire the fact that he is a fine specimen of wolf. I don't think I have ever seen a pure white wolf before. That admiration is quickly washed away by the fact he is being a possessive, idiotic dickhead. He is also more dangerous as he is caught up deep in his instincts to protect his 'true Mate'.

I am pulled from my musings as Garett roars in pain, my

eyes zeroing in on the large claw marks that have cut him across his chest. This is ridiculous. I pull on my discarded jeans and quickly do up my shirt. Me walking around half naked is not going to help anything.

"Guys, knock it off!" I shout out, trying to push some of my power into my voice.

They both ignore me and continue fighting. Garett is up on his two hind legs, swatting at the large wolf as he gets close, trying to pounce when Killian gets too close. Killian has a couple of lacerations on him, but he is carrying on like he can't feel them, Perhaps he can't, given how worked up he is. Garett, however, lets out a pained roar as the wolf bites his front paw hard, causing the bear to retreat back. Enough is enough.

I jump forward and try to put myself in between Garett and Killian. Bad idea. Killian spins towards me, locked so deep in the fight he doesn't realise it's me. He leaps towards me, teeth bared and I know I am about to get bitten. Garett roars again and swats me out of the way, taking the bite that was meant for me. The strength of Garett's push sends me flying into a chest of drawers. The pain running through my arm where I hit the furniture makes me want to cry out. Flashes of white fill my vision as the pain threatens to overwhelm me. I look at my arm to see it's bleeding and a glimpse of protruding bone tells me I've broken it. I hiss out a curse and bind my arm with whatever I can grab hold of out of the chest of drawers. I know that if I cry out, or if I stay for long and the boys scent my blood, it will distract them and make them sloppy. I don't want either of them to die today, so I need to do something about it. I am also pretty sure I am going to pass out soon so I need to get help.

Gritting my teeth, I stand up and make my way to the door, trying to avoid the two ferocious shifters who are circling around the room. I exit and hurry down the stairs as quickly as my legs will carry me. I have to lean against the wall when I reach the bottom as the room begins to spin, my vision starting to blur. I look down and see I have left a trail of blood. Shit. They may be neck-deep in fighting, but if Killian gets caught up in blood lust he will track me down. Pushing away from the wall, I stumble through the building, shoving the door open and running towards the main house. I can't see anyone around. Bloody typical. Usually I am tripping over people and now I can't find a single person when I need them. I continue to jog, my steps becoming more of a stumble as the main house comes into view.

"Ari!" a happy voice calls out.

I spin around and see Seb walking towards me with a large smile on his face, until he sees me cradling my arm and the state of my once-white shirt. I'm sure I look a sight, and from Seb's horrified expression, my guess is correct.

"Ari! What happened?" he calls out as he runs towards me, catching me as I stumble forward.

"Get Alpha Mortlock! Killian and Garett have shifted and are fighting," I say, my words tumbling out in my mouth in a hurry.

"Shit! Where are they?" he asks, frowning as he looks over me.

"My bedroom," I say, and I see a look cross his face.

Had the situation been different, he would have made a remark, but I can see him push his jokes aside as he nods solemnly at me and runs back towards the main building.

I turn around and start the journey back to the room, hurrying as quickly as I can – which, in my current state, isn't very fast. By the time I make it up the top of the stairs, I can hear pounding footsteps running towards me.

"Ari, stay back. I'm afraid your presence is only going to

make things worse," Alpha Mortlock's voice greets me, his face looking apologetic but firm. He is not going to let me in that room.

"No way, I need to check if Garett is okay," I try to bite out, but my voice comes out weak.

Alex walks up to me. I didn't even see him arrive, but he puts his hand gently on my cheek, bringing my eyes to meet his.

"Ari, you need to take care of yourself. Both of those men are going to need you later, and you can't help them if you're passed out." His comment is reasonable and it makes me groan.

He takes this as acceptance that I'm not going to barge into the fight and follow the Alpha into the room. I see a glance of shattered furniture and hear lots of growling but I don't see either of the shifters. A gentle hand touches my shoulder and I look around to see Seb smiling softly at me.

"Come on, Ari, let's get you sorted."

I follow him down the stairs and into one of the treatment rooms. Thankfully, Nurse Beth hasn't left yet. Her eyes widen as she sees me, hurrying over and gesturing for me to sit on the examination bed.

"My god, Ari, what happened?" she asks, unwrapping my arm and sucking in a deep breath as she takes in the damage.

I explain in as little detail as possible what happened, keeping out the part where Garett and I had sex, but Seb wiggles his eyebrows at me so I know he has an idea as to what we had been up to.

Several stitches later, my arm is bound up and suspended in a sling. My shifter healing has already started to kick in and I should be good as new by tomorrow. Nurse Beth has to leave, but is going to send over a colleague to help us out while I am injured. I lean against the counter in the treatment room as Seb tries to make me smile by telling me pack stories.

"–and then Alex came running in, looking like he was being chased by death hounds and had to explain to his older brother why Elder Smith was so furious," Seb tells me in between laughter.

I have to say, hearing stories about a young, impulsive Alex is taking my mind off of the current situation a little. I fight to keep back a smile at the image of the current pack Beta acting so recklessly.

"What happened to Alex's brother?" I ask. I remember meeting him when I first presented myself to the pack.

Seb sighs and rubs his hand across the back of his neck like he is uncomfortable.

"Do you remember the attack on the pack?" he asks, to which I nod in response. It's the reason I'm here, after all: their last medical staff were killed in that attack. "Well, Mark was killed during that. He was our Beta at the time. It was an assassination rather than a random attack. ASP tried to play it off as a random rogue attack, but they hit us hard by aiming for specific pack members: our medical team, both our Gamma and our Beta, a couple of the Elders. Alpha Mortlock and his mate were targeted but the Alpha managed to fight them off." Sorrow laces his voice.

"When the previous Beta died, Alpha Mortlock suggested Mark for his Beta. No one challenged it. Mark was a good Beta, he was always fair. Alex was always the more powerful of the two, but he was younger and more reckless. When Mark died, Alex stepped into the position. There were some who weren't happy with that, but they knew they wouldn't be able to beat Alex in a challenge. The death of his brother changed him. Gone was the carefree Alex that I grew up with."

I let myself digest this information; it explains some things about Alex: why one minute he is flirting with and teasing me –

a glimpse of the old Alex – and the next he is the serious Beta of the pack. I feel for him, that he had to grow up too quickly. I know how that feels.

There is a pause in the conversation and I notice that upstairs has become much quieter. There is no snarling or growling from the fighting shifters. That has to be a good sign, right? Seb realises that I am distracted and goes to make us some coffee. I am staring at the clock on the wall when Alpha Mortlock walks into the room, his face weary. I push off from the counter and race to his side.

"Is everyone okay?" I demand in a hurry.

"Nothing that a few hours sleep won't sort out. I think their pride has been injured more than their bodies. Garett is pretty torn up over your arm, though," he tells me, his face grim. "Lets go over to the gym. We need to sort this out and I think it's best if we do so where there is some space in case someone gets riled up again."

I nod in agreement.

An hour later, I am pacing the gym as I wait to get the answers I need. I would prefer to do this without so much of an audience but the Alpha insisted. The Alpha, Lena, Alex and Isa are here, along with Seb, Garett and Killian. Even Nurse Penny is here, tending to Killian's wounds. She is the nurse sent to relieve Beth from the other pack.

Garett is leaning against the gym wall, avoiding my gaze. At first I thought it was because he is angry with me, but when I see the look of anguish in his eyes I know it's because he is feeling guilty. I should probably feel bad and go to comfort him, but right now I can't process what I am feeling. Besides, it will not help the situation for me to be comforting Garett when Killian is snarling at any man that comes near me. I look across at the idiot and see he is staring at me again. Tearing his gaze from me as if it's agony to do so, he snarls at Nurse Penny, who is trying to tend to his wounds.

"I give up!" she proclaims, as she pulls away from the surly shifter. Turning to the Alpha, she shrugs her shoulders. "He won't let me treat him. All of his wounds will heal by them-selves," she explains and packs away her equipment.

"Thank you, Penny. If you could go back to the medical room in case anyone else needs you. We will call down if we need you here again," Alpha Mortlock instructs.

She nods like she was expecting this, but a slight look of disappointment fills her gaze. I bet she was hoping she would get to listen in, and report back to her Alpha. Suspicion creeps in. I will be keeping an eye on her. Mortlock meets my eyes and nods in agreement, his thoughts matching mine. Smart move to send her away.

"I can smell the bear on her," Killian growls as Nurse Penny leaves, and I fight the urge to smack him.

"Who I fuck has nothing to do with you, Killian," I retort, anger fuelling my words.

This guy really gets on my fucking nerves. I don't know what it is about him that gets under my skin so much. My wolf can't decide if she wants to fuck him or fight him. Maybe both? *Focus, Ari!*

Killian jumps up from his chair and starts to stalk towards me, a challenge in his eyes. Alex and Isa jump forward to block him from reaching me.

"You are my Mate; it has everything to do with me," he growls, his voice dropping to the point I think he is going to lose control to his wolf.

Alpha Mortlock is by his side, talking low into his ear, trying to calm him down. I can see Garett has moved away from the wall, and from his rigid stance, he looks about one comment away from shifting as well.

"I am not your fucking Mate! Just because some stupid instinct is telling you we 'belong together' does not make it true! I have not accepted the bond. I don't even know you!" I spit. My wolf is pushing against my control and my grip on my power has diminished, filling the room with Alpha power.

I can see how it is affecting Killian. His power meets mine in a rush, brushing up against me almost in a caress, feeding my power rather than fighting it. Killian's front teeth lengthen and he takes another step forward, pushing past Alex and Isa, forcing them both take a step back. The Beta and Gamma share a look. That on its own should have me worried, but I am so deep in my frustration and anger that it doesn't register.

"Are you really telling me you can't feel it? You can't feel our bond?" His words come out as a caress, his voice almost a purr as if he knows the answer already.

I want to snarl at him and tell him that I feel nothing, but that would be a lie. His power does call to me. Most Alpha power is rough and fights for dominance, but Killian's feels like it is supporting me, making me stronger. It makes my power want to do the same, and that terrifies me. I am about to lash out, out of panic, when Alpha Mortlock turns to look at me.

"Ari, pull back, you are not helping the situation by throwing around your power," he says calmly.

Had it been anyone else, it might have felt like he was scolding me, but I can tell he is just being truthful.

"Killian, you need to calm down. Ari is safe; you need to fight your instincts so we can sort this out. You are stronger than this, my friend," he says softly and I can see that this reaches Killian.

He blinks and I can see him trying to fight against his instincts, his muscles trembling. Tearing his gaze away from me, he takes deep breaths to try and regain control.

By some unspoken signal from Mortlock, Lena steps forward, wringing her hands as she comes under the gaze of us all.

"Ari, something obviously occurred between you and Garett. What I am sure you don't know is that Killian would have been able to feel your... arousal through the bond, which is what caused him to snap," she explains to me.

That explains why it looked like he had run into the room. Because he could feel me fucking another man. My face burns red as embarrassment fills me. Fan-fucking-tastic.

"So Killian is going to know every time I sleep with someone?" I ask bluntly and I can see Killian's face whip towards me. "How can I stop it?" I demand.

"The only way to stop this is to accept the bond. It is highly unusual for someone to sleep with someone else when they have found their true Mate," she says, igniting the anger in me once more.

"I can sleep with whoever I want! I don't care what some

'bond' says." I retort, and I see Lena take a step back at the venom in my words.

I will not be made to feel guilty for sleeping with Garett. Alpha Mortlock snarls slightly at the threat to his Mate before regaining his composure with a slight cough.

"Oh no! I didn't mean it like that, Ari. I just meant that once the bond has made itself clear, the two don't usually *want* to sleep with anyone else. It usually takes *years* to get past the urge to only spend time with your true Mate. If you don't accept the bond, those feelings will eventually disappear, but it takes time," she hurries to inform me, wanting to make sure that I understand that she isn't judging me.

"But I don't want a Mating bond!" I cry out.

"You think I want this?" Killian demands, pushing past Alex and Isa as he stalks towards me.

Garett snarls and Killian bares his teeth at him.

"Don't push me, Bear," he spits out, his temper barely under control. He comes within an inch of me, his eyes piercing, pinning me to the spot. "I had a Mate. What we had was real. This 'true Mated Pair' business is bullshit. You think I want to be Mated to an uncontrolled Shadowborn who barely knows how to summon her wolf? I don't." His voice starts off harsh, but towards the end frustration laces his tone. "But then why can I not seem to control myself around you?" he asks, but I know the question isn't to me.

His hand comes up to cup my cheek and I can't stop myself from leaning into the warmth of it. What the fuck is going on with me?

Chapter Seventeen

*I*t was decided that we all needed some time to cool off and figure out what everyone involved wanted. I hadn't paid Alex much attention but I felt his eyes on me the whole time, and I couldn't help feeling like I had let him down. Garett agreed not to discuss Killian's attack on him with his pack. The last thing any of us needed was an all-out war between the bears and Moon River Pack.

He almost caused a fight when he was saying goodbye though. Prowling towards me, he pulled me into his arms and kissed me soundly before walking out to the sounds of Killian's growls. He had wanted to stay but it had been decided that was not the best idea while Killian was still fighting for control. I would be having words with him about his predatory behaviour another time. It was out of character for him, but I didn't want to mention it in front of everyone after Killian had wounded his pride.

The next couple of days fell into a bit of a routine. I arrive at the compound and check on my patients. I then have an open clinic for anyone to come and ask for advice about various ailments. I am glad to throw myself into the work, into some-thing familiar, as it means that I am too busy to think over everything that has happened in the last few days. I'm not ready to deal with that just yet. In the afternoons before I leave for the day, I train with Killian. Isa is now helping with my training; it was thought that it would be best for me to have a sparring partner and someone who could break up any fights between the two of us. Isa is a much harsher sparring partner; fighting with her is like trying to throw a brick wall. Thankfully with Isa around, there have been no further 'incidents' between me and Killian. Once I finish with training for the day, tired and sore, I head back to the apartment where Tori grills me on what happened that day. She has even started to eat popcorn while I am filling her in, telling me my life is far more entertaining than any soap on TV.

I'm not sleeping very well. At night, when I no longer have anything to distract me, my thoughts keep me awake. Garett has been calling me, checking that I'm okay and that Killian is staying in line. I know that he wants to be with me and that he is fighting against his nature to stop his bear from tearing down the compound to find me. I don't regret that we slept together, but it makes it much harder to sort though my feelings for him. I like him, I do, and I can't ignore that my feelings for him are more than just of friendship, but I am scared to take things further. While bears do take mates, like with wolves, it isn't all that frequent. But when they find a partner, they tend to stay together for life and I fear that Garett is feeling that for me. I don't know if I can be that person for him.

Not to mention Killian. Even if I weren't psychologically screwed, that would throw a spanner in the works. I also can't deny that I do feel something when I am around him, but is that just because of the bond? Just some wolfy-voodoo that is forcing us to feel something for the other? I'm not even sure I like the guy, let alone want to bond with him.

Alex is also another problem I keep muddling over. When we kissed in the woods, something just clicked. It felt right when we were in our wolf form. I've gone from despising the guy to wanting to fuck him. But if I push further, my 4am thoughts whisper to me than it's more than that.

Then there is Seb. Sweet, loving Seb who always manages to put a smile on my face. He hasn't treated me differently at all or tried to make me feel guilty about what has happened. And as hard as I fight it, I keep finding myself watching him. I am developing feelings for him and I don't want to – I don't want our friendship to change in that way.

My alarm clock blares to life and I sit up in bed to switch it off. I was already awake anyway. I go through my usual routine and get ready for the day, throwing on some loose clothing. Thankfully I have fully healed now, so getting into clothes that fit isn't an issue anymore, but I asked Alpha Mortlock to provide me with a uniform so it felt more like a job. I need to keep that distinction. This is just a job and my life will return to normal once it is all over, right? We still haven't gotten to the bottom of the Shadow Pack. There have been no more attacks and no one in the supernatural community has heard anything – except for Eric and his mysterious 'friends'. I sigh as I pick up my phone and see another text from him. He has backed off a lot since our last chat, but he has been sending me updates. A large gray wolf with a scar on its face, who doesn't belong to any of the local packs, has been seen prowling around the city.

"Well, that's a coincidence," I mutter dryly to myself.

I am still no closer to working out what I am going to do about them. Since I have been training I can feel myself getting stronger, but I certainly can't take on a whole pack. A little part of me whispers that I could if I accepted my Shadowborn abilities, but I push that part deep, deep down and carry on getting ready for the day.

My morning flies by with check-ups and walk-in appoint-
ments. Lottie has fully recovered and her and her mother visit
me every morning with a fresh batch of muffins. I keep telling
them that they don't need to, but secretly I love it. I've been
seeing Sarah, the pregnant shifter, regularly as well. Her pregnancy seems to be coming along well, but now she is 36 weeks
and will be delivering soon.

Shifter pregnancies are similar to human ones; however,
most shifter babies arrive after 37–38 weeks, don't ask me why.
I never studied supernatural birthing. Female shifters also
experience a strong nesting desire just before they give birth, so
Sarah has been busy cleaning her cabin and getting it ready for
the baby. The father, Rubin, is always nervously pacing the
room when I visit. The one time Seb came with me, Rubin
chased him out of the house, his protective instincts on overdrive. This is an understandable reaction for our kind, especially as Moon River has been having problems with expectant
mothers having trouble carrying pregnancies to term, or problems with the birthing. Alpha Mortlock pulled me aside one
morning and told me that there have also been issues with
fertility as well. In fact, the last litter of healthy pups were born
over two years ago. This makes me nervous and I have
requested Nurse Beth to put me in touch with a supernatural

midwife. Mortlock won't be happy but he will have to put up with it. Babies are not my speciality and he knew that when he took me on.

I am just wiping down the examination room surfaces when I hear a cheery call of my name.

"Ari, hello dear!"

I turn and smile at the happy woman walking into the room.

"Gloria, how are you? I don't think I've seen you since the social. How is Jessica?" I ask, my smile wide and genuine.

I surprise myself when I realise that I have missed her. I only met her the once at the social, yet I feel connected to her through Seb. She makes me feel like I am welcome, even though I have caused so much trouble in her pack.

"I'm fine, dear," she replies as she takes a seat in the room, her eyes running over me. "But, how are you? Have you been sleeping? You look exhausted," she comments.

For once I find I'm not annoyed by someone 'mothering' me. In fact, I find myself smiling at the older woman, knowing she is just looking out for my best interests.

"I'm fine, Gloria, pleased to be doing some good again," I tell her with a smile, gesturing to the treatment room.

I hadn't realised how much of an effect not being able to practice would have on me, or how much nursing is ingrained into who I identify as.

"Seb told me about what's been going on with Killian and the others." Damn, I was hoping to avoid this conversation.

I sigh and am hesitant to meet her eyes, worried what I might see there. When I do, however, all I see is understanding, not even a flicker of disappointment.

"Last week was eventful," I tell her, and she chuckles at the understatement.

"So are you going to Mate with Killian?" she asks, straight to the point. That's one of the things that I love about Gloria: no messing around! She says it as she sees it.

I bite my lip. I really don't want to be having this conversation. If I say it out loud, it makes everything so much more real. Tori knows the basic details, but she doesn't understand pack politics. She thinks I should just sleep with all of them, no strings attached, but I know that won't work. Too many Alpha males with delicate egos, and if I were to sleep with Killian, I don't think we would be able to deny the mating bond. Not that I even want to sleep with him. Or maybe I do? Gah! Too many feelings, I don't know whether I'm coming or going!

"I don't even know him! Why should I tie myself to someone because some supernatural bullshit has decided that we 'belong together'? Why can't I decide for myself? He certainly doesn't seem to want to bond, he hates this!" I tell her, and I see her nod her understanding.

"Okay, so Garett then. What's happening there?" she moves on, watching me intently like my body language is telling her more than my words.

I feel a wave of sadness fill me at the change of topic. I miss Garett, but with everything going on I feel it's best we have some distance from each other. He agrees with this, although I know that he is struggling, his instincts telling him that he should be with me.

"I don't even know. We are taking some space from each other while this is going on. I miss him, though. Oh, what a mess! I don't know what to do. I don't want a relationship with him – I'm not ready for that, and I know that's what he wants," I rant, my thoughts flying around my head.

"And Alex, I know there is something going on there. Oh come now, don't pull that face at me, I know these things," she chides me, as I make a face at the topic of conversation.

"We kissed when he took me for a run," I admit, looking down at my nails as I avoid her gaze. "He is so hot and cold, though. One minute he flirts with me and the next he is distant."

Gloria nods through this and tilts her head to one side.

"Do you know about his past?" she asks, I nod my head. Seb filled me in only the other day. "Since his brother died, he changed. Some for the better, but he has distanced himself from us, and doesn't seem to know how to enjoy himself anymore. He doesn't think he deserves to. When you are around, I can see a bit of that playful little boy that used to cause havoc in my kitchen with Seb."

She pauses to let this information sink in. I take my hair down from the professional ponytail I had put it up in and run my hands through it, trying to order my thoughts. In the end, I groan and put my face in my hands.

"What a mess. I don't know what I'm going to do. How do I choose between them when I don't know what I'm feeling? Do I even want to choose? I don't want a relationship," I mutter from behind my hands.

I hear footsteps and then a gentle hand on my back, rubbing in small circles to comfort me.

"Why don't you want a relationship?" she asks softly, her hands keeping up the gentle touch on my back.

I bite my lip. How much do I tell her? I'm not sure I'm ready to face this.

"I–" I stop, my voice croaky. Clearing my throat, I start again. "I loved once. I was only young. It was more infatuation than anything..." I'm rambling. *Stop, Ari, focus.* I take a deep breath. "My old pack was harsh, their rules ultimate. He was the only one to show me comfort and he was punished for it. It was forbidden and he was taken from me." I stop, my eyes burning.

I squeeze them shut, pushing the memories away. Flashes of his face pass through my mind and I shove them away, deep down. Not today. I can't think about him today.

"Relationships only end up in pain and loss. Everyone will be taken away from me eventually. Tori and Garett are only in my life because they made such a nuisance of themselves and were so persistent that I didn't even notice when they went from acquaintances to family." I open my eyes and I'm sure that my pain is clear on my face from the expression Gloria gives me.

"Besides," I mutter, my voice dropping as I admit to my true reason, "I'm not good enough. I did some terrible things when I was in my last pack, things that you would hate me for. I am broken because of it. I can't inflict that on someone." I am whispering by the end of my admission.

I am afraid to meet Gloria's eyes, as I am sure that she will hate me for what I have told her. She will not want me anywhere near Seb. My fears are met when her hand stops its slow circles on my back.

"Were you forced to do these things? Did you choose to do them?" she asks me, her voice neutral, hiding her thoughts from me.

"No, I didn't want to do them! I fought against it, but I wasn't strong enough. It doesn't matter, though. I still did them. I am just as evil as the ones who made me do it." Despair fills me, and I am sure the pack is going to learn how broken and twisted I truly am.

My eyes fly open as arms come around me tightly and I stare down in shock at Gloria, who is hugging me fiercely, tears glistening in her eyes.

"I am so sorry that you had to go through that, and that you have felt this burden. You are not evil. You had tough decisions to make and you survived. You work so hard to help others. You deserve a chance to feel loved." She releases me from her arms and looks up at me, a small smile on her lips. "And if that happiness is with more than one person, then so what?"

I stare at her in shock. Is she really suggesting getting into a relationship with more than one guy? Alphas will struggle to share, and would never accept a bear into that mix. My head is spinning with the possibilities.

"Oh, don't look so shocked. It's not uncommon for female shifters to have more than one partner. It just doesn't happen as often as it used to. But now our numbers are so low, who knows what may happen in the future? Besides, each of those men can offer you something different. Perhaps they can help heal you," she carries on.

"Now." She pauses and I look up at her in expectation. "What about Seb?" she asks, her tone gentle and not an ounce of judgement is in her voice.

"What about him?" I ask, guilt filling my voice and my face flushing red, giving me away.

"I don't think that anything has happened between you, but Seb can't stop speaking about you. After he has seen you, he is bouncing around like when he was a cub at Christmas. I know he cares for you, and I personally would love to welcome you into our family as one of our own. But I just ask you, please don't hurt him. Don't lead him on. If you have feelings for him, then by all means, but he isn't as strong as the Alphas that are vying for your attentions. Please keep him safe," she tells me earnestly, before coming to embrace me again and kissing my cheek before walking out of the room, leaving me standing speechless.

 $\mathcal{M}$ y training session with Killian comes around all too quickly. They are going well, I am progressing fast, but sooner or later I am going to have to start training in my wolf form and I have been dreading this. Isa is the only one allowed to spar with me, as when we tried with Alex being my sparring partner, Killian nearly ripped his head off when he flipped me. He still has to fight his instincts and I can hear snarls coming from his end of the gym when I am pinned to the mats.

I walk into the gym and see him lifting weights in the back corner. His loose tracksuit bottoms do nothing to hide his muscular legs and he is shirtless, the muscles in his arms and upper body cording as he lifts the weights.

"Personally I don't tend to go for skinny guys. I prefer mine more muscular." Isa's voice comes from behind me, making me jump.

She smirks as my face flushes red at having been caught staring. I follow her into the room but can't help looking over at Killian. I can't believe Isa thinks that he is skinny; he is more muscular than most football players. I dread to think how big Isa's men are.

We start warming up and Killian walks over, wiping his forehead with his towel as he does so.

"Decided to show up?" he asks me, his eyebrow raised.

"Of course I did. Why wouldn't I? I've been here every day this week!" I reply indignantly.

"You made such a fuss yesterday that I thought we might have broken you. Delicate little princess," he smirks. He knows I hate it when he calls me that.

"Stop being such a dick, Killian. Let's get this over with," I say tiredly.

He frowns at me as he looks me over. "Why are you so tired? Are you not sleeping?"

"Since when do you care?" I ask, no venom in my voice. I actually want to know the answer.

He goes still and looks me over again, an expression I can't describe passing over his face.

"I do care. I just wish I didn't," he answers quietly, before walking to the edge of the mats. "Right, stop standing around. Get to it!" he shouts.

Isa has been looking back and forth between the two of us and if I wasn't so thrown by Killian's comment, it might have been comical.

The first hour of training goes as usual, but because I'm so tired, I keep making mistakes.

"Come on, Ari, even a five-year-old could get out of that hold," Killian calls from the side of the mats.

I am pinned to the floor once again and my temper is starting to rise. I should be used to his taunts by now, and I have to admit that he isn't as harsh as he used to be, but lack of sleep is making me cranky.

Isa lets me out of the hold and I push from the ground angrily. Killian watches my display of temper in silence, arms crossed with a contemplative look on his face.

"Lets change this up. Shift into wolf form," he shouts out.

My head whips round to look at him, my body stiffening up at his command. "No," is all I say.

"I said, shift," he snarls, our tempers setting each other off.

"And I said NO. I will not shift." Not today, not when I am in this mood and not in front of Killian.

"What is your problem? I thought you Shadowborn relished that opportunity to shift and show off your powers? *Shift*," he orders again, embedding his Alpha power into his words.

My knees buckle, but not from his power. Memories flash before my eyes and I am dragged under.

"Shift." The command comes at me again.

I shake my fifteen-year-old head, but not out of teenage attitude. I stare up at the Alpha and bare my teeth.

"No." My voice croaks and my body aches from the punishment I received earlier in the week.

The fact that my shifter body had not yet healed my wounds just goes to show how badly they beat me. After I escaped with Zack's help, they held a much tighter leash on me, and the beating I had received when they dragged me back was the worst so far. Had I been human, I would have died. Now that Zack was dead, I had no one to tend to my wounds under the cover of darkness. My heart threatens to break at the thought of the only wolf who ever showed me kindness losing his life because of me.

A boot kicks me in the back and I cry out as I fall forward before, pushing myself back up onto my knees, glaring at the Alpha and my tormentor. I don't care how much they beat me; I will no longer do as they ask. Any misplaced loyalty to them was lost the moment they killed Zack.

"I said, shift," the Alpha repeats, his voice full of Alpha power.

I fall forward onto all fours once again as his power forces the change in me. He doesn't need to raise his voice; his power will make me do as he wishes. I know that resisting is futile, but I can't just roll over and do as he says, so I fight it. The change is painful and once again I hate that he has this power over me; that I am a wolf, a preda-tor, but I can't stop him from controlling me.

Eventually I find myself looking at my paws, panting, and I hear him walk forward. He drops his hand to the scruff of my neck and I flinch as he pats me.

"Well done, little wolf. I have a job for you."

I come back around to Killian calling my name, his hands on my shoulders as he anxiously looks at me. Wait, Killian looks anxious? Scratch that, now that he has seen me come around, his face has dropped back into his customary scowl, but I can see the worry in his eyes.

"What happened? What triggered you?" he asks, but I get the feeling he already knows.

"You forcing me to try and shift," I mutter, running my hand across my face.

I only notice then that my hands are shaking. Killian notices too and swears under his breath.

"Isa, we are going to stop for the day. Ari, come for a walk with me," he tells me, and his tone sounds resigned.

Isa looks between the two of us again like she can't decide what is happening or whether to allow this. This time, it does make me crack a smile.

"Go, I will be fine," I say. "If he tries to seduce me, I will just hit him over the head like you showed me," I tell her with a wink.

This makes her laugh and she walks out of the gym, leaving just me and Killian. I turn to look at the shifter and find him putting on a shirt. Shame. He catches me looking and raises an eyebrow at me again, desire heating his eyes before he shuts it down. I just shrug.

"So, where are we going?" I ask, hoping that my nerves at being alone with him don't come through in my voice.

"Into the woods. Come," is all he says before walking off.

I can't help but wonder if this walk is going to be anything like the last time I went into the woods with a wolf shifter, when I ended up making out with Alex. Part of me hopes it does.

"Why are we here?" I ask as we stare out at the trees.

Killian has brought me to a small clearing in the middle of the woods. We are close enough that I can still hear the hubbub of the main house, but far enough away that no one will be able to overhear our quiet conversation. I am sitting on a log watching the small birds hunt for grubs in the undergrowth. Killian is sitting on the other end of the log, and I can feel that his gaze keeps landing on me.

"We need to talk. About the bond. And about you," he tells me, and I sigh.

This is another conversation I really don't want to have, but he is right: we do need to talk. We can't keep avoiding the issue.

"Fine. What do you want to know?" I ask, finally meeting his gaze.

"Why do you keep rejecting the bond?" he asks, and I can hear a slight note of vulnerability in his voice.

I am surprised and I'm sure it shows on my face. "Are you saying you want this bond? I thought you hated me!" I state incredulously. I can't get a true reading on this guy!

Frustration fills his face and he pushes away from the log, prowling through the clearing. If I didn't know that he was a shifter, I would still be able to tell he was something 'other' with the power rolling off him. His sharp features almost make him look Fae-like.

"I don't hate you! I hate what you are!" he snarls as he paces.

I feel like he has poured a bucket of ice over me. Shadowborn. Even when I feel I am making a life for myself elsewhere, it still follows me. I can never escape it. I stand up stiffly, trying to hide the hurt from his comment.

"Well, I can't do anything to change that. I hate that you're such a bastard but that's not going to change either. Guess both of us are going to be disappointed," I retort and spin to leave the clearing.

I am not going to sit here and listen to him insult me. I thought we were going to chat and finally work out what's going on, but it seems I am going to be disappointed. I hear Killian's footsteps pause and a curse under his breath.

"Ari, wait. I'm not doing this very well. You rile me up and I forget what I'm trying to say," he admits.

I turn around and raise my eyebrow at him and his shitty apology. But I can see from his posture that he is not used to doing this. Sighing, I sit back down and look at him expectantly.

"I'm not going to apologise for being Shadowborn," I tell him, my voice strong on this point. I wish I hadn't been born this way, but there is nothing I can do to change that.

"I know. Let me try and explain." He sits back down on the log and turns so he is facing me. "I was Mated before. Julie and I chose to be bonded, and I meant those vows when I took them. We loved each other. She was kind and gentle and never had a bad word to say about anyone." His voice is soft as he tells me about her, and I realise I've never seen him like this.

"A couple of wolves from another pack came to petition for a place of safety. Something was off about them, but I decided to offer them a place in the pack, against the judgement of my Beta and Gamma. They didn't really fit within the pack and several members came to convince me to ask them to leave. I declined. I was trying to be more accepting. A month later, there was an attack on the pack during the night. Someone had let them in the compound and had told them where to strike to cause the most damage. It was a complete slaughter," he tells me, his voice hard.

He stops and takes a deep breath, his hands clenching together and I have to fight the urge to stroke his back in comfort.

"I ran back to our house and found one of the wolves I had granted a place of safety within the pack at my bedside. His hands were wrist deep in my Mates stomach as he pulled her apart bit by bit. He was Shadowborn, and half in his shadow form at the time. Julie hadn't even heard him coming." His voice is soft, broken, and I can see unshed tears in his eyes.

I go to place my hand on his arm, but his gaze sharpens.

"That is what was off about that wolf. He was Shadowborn. He infiltrated my pack, betrayed us and then killed them all. I managed to kill most of them, but I have a feeling they left me alive on purpose. As a message."

He turns to look at me now, and I can see his eyes soften a little as he looks at me, although I can still feel the anger within him.

"That's why I knew you were Shadowborn. I also had some training from my predecessor on how to teach them. We had a Shadowborn in our pack about 150 years ago, so we pass the knowledge down, in case another is born." He seems to realise his use of the present tense and lets out a tired sigh. "Not that I have anyone to pass that knowledge to anymore. My pack is dead."

He shifts his weight on the log and turns to face me fully, his knee bumping against me as he runs his eyes over me again, taking in every detail.

"Fate has a sick sense of humour. I had a mate and that love was real. And now it has brought me to you, the very same kind that killed her. You are nothing like Julie. I shouldn't want anyone else." He pauses and I can hear the self-loathing in his voice. "But I feel complete when you are around, like I might have a reason to still be alive. When Julie and the pack were killed, I wondered why the world was so cruel. I should have died with them. Protecting them. Since then I have been living a half-life, not truly belonging. Perhaps fate led me to you so you could mend the rift in my heart." His words are soft, uncertain, like he is laying his heart out for me to see.

I stare at him with wide eyes and panic. I jump to my feet and start pacing in front of the log. He can't possibly think that I can fix him. *Me!* I let out a slightly manic laugh as I pace.

"I am the most broken person here!" I practically shout at him, my nerves getting the better of me.

My fight-or-flight instincts are screaming for me to leave, but I know I can't get out of having this conversation.

"I am not a good person. I don't belong anywhere. You said it yourself: I am nothing like Julie! I have killed. The things I was made to do should make you want to kill me. Hell, I probably deserve to be ripped to shreds! What I don't deserve is a fated Mate!" My voice is loud and I can hear my panicked breaths coming out fast. I'm sure my eyes are bright with tears that threaten to fall. All my carefully built walls are being torn down by these guys and leaving the scared, damaged little girl that is hiding behind it. Exposed.

Killian watches my little breakdown in silence, but now he stands up and prowls towards me. I can't work out what is in his expression, but he doesn't look like he is going to kill me like I suggested.

"Ari." He says my name and pulls me to a stop when he gets close enough. Putting his hand on the tops of my arms, he looks me in the eyes. They look warm. "I have my dark side, too: things I am ashamed of. I know that you are different from the Shadowborn that killed my pack, and I know I don't always show it very well, but I don't blame you for things you were forced to do. Perhaps we were brought together to help fix each other. I don't belong anywhere either. I don't have a place here and I don't have a place to call home, and I didn't expect to have that again after I lost Julie. But when I am with you, that feels like it could be a possibility again."

Huh. Who knew Killian had a romantic side?

"I know it's not going to be easy, but I'm working on my prejudices. Sometimes, I see your strength and it scares me, but I've seen how you push yourself to help others. I know you're not like him," he tells me, raising one of his hands to cup my cheek.

I take a deep breath and fight the urge to lean into his hand as I gather my thoughts and brace myself for the backlash of what I am about to say.

"I do feel drawn to you. Your power speaks to me and I feel connected to you, somehow, in a way I never have before. But I am also drawn to Garett and Alex, and even Seb. I don't know if I can commit to this bond when I have feelings for other people as well. There is something deeper going on here." I bite down on my lower lip as I wait for his response.

He pulls away and is silent for a while. A frown mars his face making his scar look more severe.

"I don't like it. It goes against who I am," he tells me, and I brace myself for rejection. "But I have decided to trust my instincts more. I should have trusted them that night the Shadowborn asked for shelter, and I didn't. My instincts are telling me this is right." He pauses again and paces the clearing.

I can tell that he is struggling with this, and the fact he is even considering giving us a chance makes me see him in a different light. I can't deny any longer that I have feelings for him, and it seems he has come to the same conclusion.

"So, if you are saying you're being pulled towards these other men as well as me..." His voice trails off in a growl as he fights against his instincts. "Then I will trust you. Just don't expect me to be happy about sharing you."

With that shocking declaration, he leans down and smashes his lips to mine. His lips are firm and as I open mine to kiss him back, he bites down on my lower lip, making me gasp. He pulls away and I can see the lust in his eyes, his Alpha power rising and coaxing mine as they push against each other.

"I've been wanting to do that for days," he growls out, before stalking back to the main compound.

I stand dumbstruck as I watch him walk away, my hand going to my bruised lips. My wolf is demanding that I follow him and finish what he started, but I know I won't be able to stop myself from claiming him. I take a deep breath to calm myself. *Take things slow, Ari.* I shake my head and let out a small laugh. What an afternoon. I start the walk back to the medical building. Time to get back to work. But first, a cold shower.

Chapter Nineteen

I am standing by the front gates of the compound, my foot tapping excitedly, as I hear the sounds of a car coming along the driveway towards me. The black limo turns around the corner and I press the buzzer to make the electric gates open, allowing the car entrance. Normally, the limo would take guests to the main house, but I am so excited to see the limo's passenger that I took the short walk down to the gate. The back door flings open and the car screeches to a halt. I laugh at the disgruntled expression of the driver as Tori leaps out of the back and throws herself at me.

It has been a week since the disastrous training session with Killian, and it was decided that it was best for me to stay on the compound. Not for any 'mating' reasons, but because mysterious attacks on shifters have started happening. They have not been linked to the Shadow Pack, but it was decided it would be best overall. And with Sarah about to give birth at any moment, I wanted to be available when that happened.

Tori understood and even agreed with the reasoning behind me staying here, but I have missed my best friend. I had offered to try to get her a room here but she declined, saying the attacks were only on shifters so she would be safe. Besides, her magic would protect her. I managed to convince her to come to the compound for the weekend though. She has been bugging me to introduce her to my 'hot shifter toy boys' and there is a pack social tonight, so this is the perfect opportunity.

Getting her officially invited was easier than I expected. There is a lot of animosity between wolves and witches, from a feud that spans back generations. The two species used to work together in harmony; each wolf pack had a witch who would work to protect and heal them. One witch was not able to save an Alpha's mate and was killed as a result. The witch councils then recalled their members from all packs; even if they didn't want to leave, they had no choice. This resulted in the death of many sick or injured wolves who were no longer protected. The wolves have never forgiven the witches for this, and the witches never forgot the slight against their fallen sister. I saw this myself when I asked Alex whether they had a witch working for the pack. Some packs have moved past this and have some covenless witches working for them, but this is not common.

Which was why I was surprised when I requested that Alpha Mortlock allow Tori to come and stay, and he agreed. I was even more surprised when he suggested she come to the pack social. This was a time for family and togetherness. To invite a witch to this makes a statement. It has raised my opinion of him even more. Alex was not too happy, but he trusts my judgement of people and knows I would not invite Tori if I thought she would harm anyone here.

I focus on a squealing Tori and hug her back tightly. We wave the limo on. It will take Tori's bags to my room, where she will be staying while she is here.

"Come on, I'll show you around," I tell her with a grin on my face.

We leisurely walk up to the main house in the centre of the compound, arms linked as Tori talks excitedly about everything she has been doing this week. She has told me all this in our nightly phone calls, but I'm enjoying spending time in her company so much that I don't mind.

"Girl, I can see why you're staying here – this place is huge!" We have reached the main house by now and I'm showing her over to the medical centre. A couple of people have already stopped to greet us with warm smiles. "And there is plenty of eye candy to keep you entertained. Not that you need any more men to add to your harem!" she jokes and I nudge her, hissing at her to keep her voice down. But I can't help but laugh. I haven't realised how much I've missed having her around.

I keep the tour of the medical building brief before taking Tori up to my room. There are a couple of guest rooms up here, but she will be staying with me.

"It's a slumber party like you see in the movies!" She laughs and jokingly throws a pillow at me.

I throw it back at her, laughing. Neither of us have ever had a slumber party, our childhoods not allowing for it. After a bit more messing around, I help Tori settle in. We decide to start getting changed for the social, which starts in an hour. I watch Tori as she pulls on a white playsuit with a little black belt. The colour shows off her beautiful dark skin and the belt accentuates her generous curves. Her mixed heritage has blessed her with gorgeous curly dark hair that I have always been secretly jealous of.

"So," she begins, looking at me through the mirror as she adjusts the belt on her outfit. "Any updates on Killian?"

I sigh and walk towards the wardrobe where I am storing my clothes. I pull out a simple red blouse with a plunging neckline and hold it against myself, looking in the mirror.

"I don't really know, Tor. He takes every opportunity to touch me, especially when the others are around, but as soon as we are alone, he bolts. He is so on and off it's giving me whiplash," I say, before shaking my head and pulling off my top.

I pull the shirt on and do up the buttons, smoothing down the fabric as I look in the mirror. It shows off my figure nicely, with more cleavage than I would normally show. My tight jeans are on and I know these make my legs and butt look good.

"What do you think? Too much?" I ask, biting on my lower lip as I wait for her response.

"Girl, you look hot! You are going to have those guys fighting over you by the end of the evening," she says approvingly.

"I don't want them fighting over me!" I protest.

"Whatever you say, Ari," she says, her tone clearly saying she doesn't believe me as she rolls her eyes.

I sit in front of the vanity mirror and start putting on my make-up, paying more attention to it than I would usually. Pausing as I look at my reflection in the mirror, I wonder why I'm making more of an effort tonight. I tell myself it's because Tori is here and it's nice to dress up.

We joke and gossip for a bit before there is a knock on the door.

"Come in!" we both chorus, throwing a grin at each other as we do so.

Seb walks in and leans against the doorframe as he takes us in, whistling appreciatively. A sultry grin spreads across his face.

"Be still my beating heart. You both look beautiful this evening," he greets us smoothly.

Tori grins and pretends to fan herself, loving the attention.

"Now who is this piece of hot stuff? I wouldn't mind a roll in the sheets with you," she comments with a cheeky grin. Typical Tori.

I feel a rush of jealousy run through me at the comment, but I can't really blame her, Seb is looking fine this evening. His dark blue shirt is tight against his muscled torso, the colour showing off his tanned skin.

"I would be only happy to oblige your wish," Seb replies, a teasing glint in his eyes as he stalks towards Tori.

I know they are only joking and that Seb can't resist flirting with everyone and anyone, but jealousy fills me again and a wave of possessiveness makes me walk forward and place my hand on his shoulder.

"Tori, this is Seb. Seb, Tori," I introduce them, my voice tighter than I intended.

Tori raises her eyebrows at me and Seb takes my hand, grinning as he squeezes it gently. Damn, guess I didn't hide it very well. I have no right to be possessive of him. We are nothing but friends, but seeing the two of them flirting like that stirred something inside me. Pushing it aside, I give them an apologetic smile.

"Ready to go meet the pack?"

As we walk into the hub, I can't help but remember the last pack social I attended. It had started out great, and I had found that I actually enjoyed myself. Until Marcus, the dickhead, had spoiled the whole thing by challenging me. Nothing has been heard from him since he was banished. There was a little backlash from it – a few of his friends had chosen to leave the pack – but apart from that, things had settled down nicely.

I take Tori to the front of the room where Alpha Mortlock is waiting with Lena, Alex and Isa. I smile at them and pull Tori to my side.

"Alpha, Luna. This is Victoria Smith, Tori, my best friend," I introduce formally.

Alpha Mortlock smiles at me before nodding towards Tori. Lena is beaming and practically oozing happiness.

"Tori, welcome to Moon River Pack. You are a guest here and I hope you will be made to feel welcomed by me and my own," he replies back formally. "Which coven do you belong to?"

"None. I'm a bit of a misfit and don't really fit with any coven," Tori replies happily. She is proud of her differences and always describes the covens as nosy bitches.

Mortlock and Lena laugh and nod. "I think you will fit in well here then," Lena offers with a smile towards me. I roll my eyes but give her a small smile so she knows I'm not offended by her joke.

Alpha Mortlock stands up on the stage and begins welcoming everyone to the social. Alex pulls me aside and whispers to me.

"I've hardly seen you all week, Killian always seems to be with you. How are you?" he asks quietly. I can tell there is more he wants to say, but he doesn't have time. "I've got to go on stage but save me a dance later, alright?" he says with a wink before walking off.

"What was that about?" Tori whispers to me, and I shush her as people are looking our way. I'll fill her in later.

"You have probably already heard, but we have a guest on the compound. She is a witch but she has been approved by me to be here," the Alpha announces. There are several mutters in the crowd to which he now speaks.

"She is like family to our honorary pack mate, Ari, so I expect you to show her the same respect. Know that I would not allow anyone here who wishes us harm. Ari vouches for her, and I trust that. Enjoy your evening," he announces, before stepping off the stage with Alex and Isa in tow.

I remain where I am in shock. Since when did I become an honorary member of the pack? For him to announce that he trusts my judgement in front of the whole pack is a big deal. Not to mention that I notice many in the crowd nodding in agreement when he mentions my name. I am blown away by this show of support.

I snap out of my stupor when Tori pulls on my arm. I smile at her and start guiding her through the crowd.

"Come on, I want to introduce you to some people," I tell her with a wide smile.

An hour or so passes with lots of laughter and food. Gloria immediately takes to Tori and welcomes her with a large hug. Tori is just as shocked at the instant acceptance as I was when I met Gloria, having never had a mother figure growing up. Seb introduces her to all his friends and even Alex comes over for a chat. I can't see Killian, but I know he is around here; something tight in my chest tells me he is close. This new development started yesterday, like some sort of freaky homing beacon.

"Miss Tori, may I trouble you for a dance?" one of the young shifters asks Tori. Mark, I think his name is.

Tori smiles widely at him and takes his hand, walking out onto the dance floor. I struggle to hide my smile; Mark doesn't know what he is in for. Tori's dance style is... eccentric.

I am sitting with Gloria and Jessica, watching Seb chatting with his friends. Jessica is sitting in my lap, making me braid her hair when Alex comes over.

"Ari, I've come to claim my dance," he says with a smirk, holding his hand out.

Jessica jumps out of my lap and I stand, taking his offered hand. Butterflies twist my stomach and I wonder why I'm so nervous about dancing with Alex. At least it's a lively song and we won't have to slow-dance. As if he can hear my thoughts, the DJ changes the song, a slow tempo filling the air. I glare over in his direction. Typical. Alex pulls me closer, a smug smile on his lips as he holds me close to him. Suspicions rise.

"Did you have anything to do with the song change?" I ask, raising my eyebrows.

"I have no idea what you're talking about," he says with mock innocence.

Yeah, right. I snort, shaking my head as he starts leading me in a slow dance. After a while, I lose myself in the rhythm of the movement and rest my cheek against his chest. He hums happily, his hand pulling me a little closer.

"Ari," he begins, and I look up to see he is looking anxious. "I've got something that I need to tell–" He is cut off when a looming shadow appears over my shoulder.

"Can I cut in?" a voice asks, the tone more a demand than a question.

I know before I turn around that it's Killian, from the little spark in me that has lit up. Alex is stiff in my arms and I know that he is agitated.

"We are in the middle of something," Alex tells him, his voice firm as his arms tighten around me.

"I'm sure that can wait," Killian replies, his voice deep, and I feel his power start to rise. I'm worried that the two of them are going to start a fight in the middle of the social. Time to defuse the situation.

I turn around and look at Killian, crossing my arms as I look at him expectantly.

"Do we have a problem here?" I ask in a tone to match his.

"It's fine, Ari, I'll catch you later," Alex mutters and I know he must be swallowing his pride to back down to Killian.

Alex stalks off and I turn to glare at Killian. He puts his arms around me and I ignore the feeling of wholeness as he starts moving to the music.

"What was that all about?" I ask, my tone demanding answers.

"Alex and I had words. We have come to an agreement," he states, not even having the decency to look embarrassed at his behaviour.

"What type of agreement?" I ask through gritted teeth. Wait. "Do I even want to know?"

"Probably not." He shakes his head, a small smile playing on his lips.

We spend the rest of the dance in silence but it's a comfortable silence, even though I'm still annoyed at him. I know that shouting at Killian isn't going to get him to change or apologise, so there is no point. Unless he really pisses me off, that is. Once the dance has finished, he walks with me back to where I was sitting.

The rest of the evening passes quickly in laughter and happiness. I don't see much of Tori, who spends most of the evening on the dance floor in Mark's arms. When I finally retire to my bed, Tori doesn't join me. Instead, she decides to warm someone else's bed.

Chapter Twenty

ori slinks back to my room at around ten the next morning, looking like the cat who got the cream.

"Good night?" I ask with a sly grin as I wiggle my eyebrows.

She laughs and nods her head, her cheeks heating in a blush. My mouth drops open at the sight. Tori never blushes.

"Oh my god, you like him!" I accuse, as a large grin spreads across my face.

Tori groans and face-plants on my bed, pulling a pillow and throwing it at me.

"Yeah, and if you tell anyone I will turn you into a frog," she threatens half-heartedly.

"So... Tell me all the details," I demand, needing to know what had kept my friend's attention all night.

"We didn't sleep together if that's what you're asking. We just stayed up and talked all night... Okay, maybe a lot of kissing, but we didn't move past third base," she tells me with a laugh, the blush spreading further across her cheeks.

We spend the next hour giggling and gossiping like schoolgirls as we get ready for the day. I love spending time with Tori like this, and I can't remember the last time we did.

"So, Ari." I turn from the dresser where I'm brushing my hair to look at her, raising my eyebrow. I know that tone of voice; it means she wants something. "I know we were going to spend the day together, but do you mind if I spend some time with Mark?"

My heart sinks a little. I was hoping to spend the day with her. I have arranged for Nurse Beth to come to the compound so I could have some time off with Tori. But, looking at her face, I find that I can't tell her no. She looks so excited. I smile and nod my head.

"Oh, alright then. But I'll see you this evening, right?" I say, trying to keep my voice light.

"Of course! What are you going to do with yourself?" she asks, and I know she feels guilty from her uncertain tone of voice.

I think about it, a whole day to myself. "Don't worry about me. Enjoy yourself."

I get a sense of déjà vu as I sit in the coffee shop waiting to meet Eric. Just after Tori left to see Mark, I was pondering what to do with my unexpected free time when I received a phone call from him. He sounded pretty rough and had practically begged me to meet him. I'm still mad at him, but being the bleeding heart that I am, I caved in and agreed to see him.

I take a sip of my latte as I glance around the shop. It's a Sunday morning so it's reasonably busy, the hum of conversation in the air, and the chink of china cups settles me with its normalcy. I like coming here, or at least I did before everything kicked off with the packs. I like watching the humans go on with their day-to-day lives, oblivious to everything that is going on around them.

The bell above the door chimes to announce someone has entered the coffee shop and I glance up. Someone is hurrying towards me and throws themselves into the chair opposite me. I raise my eyebrows in question until I realise that the person is Eric. He looks appalling. His usually neat hair is all messed up and he has a couple of day's worth of stubble on his usually clean-shaven face. But the thing that shocks me the most is how pale and gaunt he looks. Dark circles mar the underside of his eyes and he looks like he hasn't slept in a week.

"Eric, what's happened to you? Are you alright?" I ask, concern lacing my voice as I place my hand on top of his. What on earth has happened to make him look like this?

He sighs and rubs his hand across his face, looking like he is going to just fall asleep where he is sitting.

"I'm fine, Ari, it's you I'm worried about," he says as his eyes run over me hungrily.

"What do you mean? I'm fine, I'm staying with a local pack that is keeping me safe," I tell him, confused at his fear for my well-being. "What has happened to you?" I ask again, I may be pissed off at him, but I still care for him.

"Look, it doesn't matter about me. There are some really dangerous people looking for you." His voice has increased in volume with his frustration and I glance around the room to make sure no one is obviously listening.

"You told me this before and nothing has happened–"

"No, Ari, listen to me. Something is about to happen, some-thing bad. You need to leave the pack and run." He tells me, leaning out of his chair towards me, grasping onto my hand like it's his lifeline.

I snort at his comment. I am not running, not after I have built a life for myself here and am just starting to feel like I fit in. There is movement around me but I am focusing only on our conversation.

"I am not running anywhere. What do you know about the pack, you need to tell me–" I am cut off as a shadow crosses the table.

I look up and see two tall men in suits. They both look like they have walked off of a fashion runway. The one closest to me smiles, and it's the kind of smile I would expect if a crocodile could grin, the one that makes you want to run.

"Ariana Blake. We are from ASP. You are going to need to come with us."

I am in deep shit. My eyes run over the small interrogation room I am currently sitting in. It's like every cop movie I have ever seen, and if it weren't me that was in trouble, I would find it amusing. At least I'm not in cuffs. I look around the sparse room, a one-way mirror fills one side of the room and the table and chair that I am sitting at are plain. A recording device sits at one end of the table. I lean back against my chair and try to think of a way out of this. The issue is that I don't know why I have been brought in. Is this the threat that Eric came to warn me about?

The sound of the door opening brings me out of my thoughts. The two men from the coffee bar walk in, their black suits accentuating their forms. One is a little taller than the other, but other than that, the two could be related. Both have black hair, although the taller one has stubble and his hair is longer. The shorter of the two is clean-shaven and, although his eyes are grey like his partner, his are softer. They both sit on the opposite side of the table and the taller of the two clears his throat.

"I am Ryan Cross and this is Aiden Cross. We are Agents for ASP and we have some questions for you," Ryan tells me, his eyes running over me as he speaks.

I nod in response to what they are saying. Same surname. I am right; they are related somehow. If I know what is good for me, I will keep my mouth shut and just respectfully answer their questions and be out of here in no time.

"You are a hard woman to get hold of. I have been trying to find you at your workplace and your apartment for a while now. Your roommate told me you had moved out," Ryan tells me.

Well, that explains who has been coming to the apartment, then. Tori's instincts reckoned they didn't mean me harm, so this should be interesting.

"So which one of you is the good cop?" I ask. Apparently I don't know what's good for me. I nod toward Aiden. "I reckon you're the good cop," I drawl, before looking to Ryan, who has a slight smile across his handsome face. "Because you have bad written all over you," I say as I lean back in my chair.

"Please don't mistake us for human police, Miss Blake. We

don't follow the same rules as them and are not restricted by human squeamishness. We will do what we need to do, to get the answers we need." He finishes on a slight growl, his smile still in place.

I am not impressed by his show of dominance, but he has just confirmed for me that he is shifter. Their scents are off and I can't quite tell what they are, but now I know what Agent Ryan is. Wolf. Which means that's what Aiden is too. Although – that doesn't feel completely right. Frowning, I look across at Aiden, who has yet to say anything. I lean forward and take a sniff, not embarrassed in the slightest, leaning back in my seat once I pick up his scent and look between the two of them.

"Bird? How can you be a bird shifter when he is a wolf? You're related, right?" I ask, briefly forgetting my current position.

It should be impossible for them to be related if they are from different shifter species. Some shifters choose to mate with a different race, but they have never been able to produce offspring, interbreeding doesn't allow reproduction. The two agents look at each other with a smile, like they are sharing a joke with each other.

"Cousins," Aiden confirms, speaking for the first time since he entered the room, his voice soft and quiet.

"But that's impossible," I argue. They must be lying, although I should be able to tell if they are lying.

"You would know about impossible," Ryan says, before leaning towards me, his eyes predatory. "For example, a Shadowborn being born and surviving under the radar for 24 years, six of those years right under our nose in the USA."

Shit.

I raise my eyebrow and pray they don't hear my heart rate spike or see the bead of sweat that is threatening to roll down the back of my neck. They can't know for definite, otherwise I wouldn't be sitting here with them like this. They would have killed me on the spot.

"That is impossible, Agent Cross. I've heard there hasn't been one of those in over 100 years, plus they don't tend to live long. I don't fancy meeting one, to be honest. I hear they are pretty nasty," I say with a shrug, trying to keep my tone light.

"We have been informed that you are a Shadowborn. Do you know a Marcus Oswald?" Ryan tells me and my blood goes cold.

Bloody Marcus. For fuck's sake, I knew I should have killed him. However, he may have given me an out.

"I wouldn't believe anything that scumbag says. He challenged me while I was a guest at Moon River Pack. I won and chose to spare him." I see both their eyebrows go up as I mention that I spared Marcus. "He was then banished from the pack for challenging a guest. I haven't seen him since. He is sore that I got him kicked out and is now out to get me." The two shifters exchange looks. They can sense that I am telling the truth, every single word ringing true. "I can't believe the bastard came running to you guys." I shake my head, my tone disgusted that he had ratted me out.

"He didn't come to us. He has been selling the information to anyone with a bit of money. We picked the information up from one of our usuals who had overheard a conversation between him and a member of the Shadow Pack. One of their members has been skulking around the city causing problems. We would have brought him in but he always seems to disappear every time we turn up. Remind me, Ariana, you were from Shadow Pack originally, right?" he asks, and I can see the moment that he picks up on my fear.

What was Marcus doing, talking to the Shadow Pack, and

why were they still here? It's not like them to hang around; they are usually all action. The fact that they are holding back makes me more nervous.

"If you are in danger, we can offer you protection," Aiden offers.

I find this odd. If they think I am Shadowborn, why are they offering me protection? I'm getting confused and frankly it's giving me a headache.

"Look boys, what's going on? Why am I here?" I ask, trying to keep my tone even.

"We want to hire you. We need someone with your... abilities." Ryan answers for me and I lean back in shock.

ASP wants a Shadowborn. I don't even want to think about what they would use those powers for, but ASP doesn't have the best reputation. They are known more for 'shoot now, talk later', and their justice is brutal, even for shifters.

"I'm not Shadowborn," I proclaim.

"Liar," Ryan call me out. Damn shifter senses!

"Do you have any proof?" I ask, knowing that they don't, as they would have used it against me already.

Both agents look at each other and I know they have nothing against me. I smile and push up from the table.

"It's been wild, boys, but I have a busy afternoon ahead of me and I need to get going." Both agents stand up with me, Ryan with a pissed-off look on his face and Aiden looks like he wants to say something else. A thought occurs to me. "Oh, my friend from the coffee bar?"

"We sent your friend on his way. We don't want to involve humans in our business," he says, confirming my suspicions that even ASP doesn't know what Eric is. Hell, if even ASP doesn't know what he is, there is no way I am going to, so this makes me feel a little better. A hand stops my path to the door when it lands on my shoulder.

"Will you consider our offer?" Ryan asks, his hand tightening on my shoulder.

"I'm sure a Shadowborn would love to join your team. Shame that's not me," I tell him, giving him a simple smile.

Ryan growls at me and stalks out of the room. What did he expect, that I would jump on his offer? I have been hiding who I am all my life. That is the only reason I am still alive today. I shake my head at him and go to walk away. Aiden stops my exit from the room with a gentle hand on my elbow, lowering his voice to the point where I have to strain my ears to hear him.

"Protect your pack. Something is coming."

My eyes widen at his words of warning. I don't bother to explain that I am only a guest and I don't belong with the pack. I nod and hurry out of the room. I need to get back and speak with the Alpha.

"Ari, the offer of protection is still there. Shadowborn or not," he calls out.

I smile at him gratefully over my shoulder, hoping that he can tell how appreciative I am at the warning.

"I'll keep that in mind!" I call out, before hurrying out of the building. He may be wrong, but Eric said something about the pack earlier as well. I need to warn the pack. Too much has been happening around the city for this to be a coincidence.

Chapter Twenty-One

$\mathcal{I}$ lay tossing and turning in bed, my thoughts stuck on the events of the day. I requested a meeting with Alpha Mortlock as soon as I got back to the compound. They wanted it to be just the Alpha, Beta, Gamma and me, but I insisted that Seb and Killian be included, as I wanted them to know everything. Everyone was quiet while I explained everything, except for Killian and Alex growling when I told them that ASP had taken me in for questioning. Even Mortlock bared his teeth when he heard this. Apparently if ASP takes a shifter into custody, they have to allow the Alpha of that pack in the interrogation room. However, ASP doesn't need to do this if the suspect is a lone wolf. There is a grey area when it comes to guests of a pack. But Moon River believes that the Alpha should have been present, especially in my case. I am still blown away that they care enough to help fight my battles. I hadn't even thought of calling the Alpha to help me.

I sent Eric a simple message letting him know I was safe and with friends, as I know he would be worried about me. I roll over for what feels like the fiftieth time and hit my pillow to make it more comfortable – when I hear an odd sound. Like footsteps, but many of them. I rack my brain. As far as I'm aware, there isn't a pack run organised for tonight, and I'm sure I would have been told if there was. I get up from my bed to walk to the window. Yes, it's definitely footsteps I can hear. Suspicion start rising through me as I reach the windows, squinting my eyes I gasp as I see around 20 wolves I don't recognise running through the compound. I hear a scream coming from the other side of the main house, which has me running for the stairs.

I sprint down the staircase and rush through the front door of the medical wing. There are wolves everywhere and it's difficult to tell who is who in the dark, especially as I haven't seen many of the pack in wolf form. I will have to do this off scent alone, which is going to make it difficult for me. I don't want to harm anyone from Moon River, and I am going to have to get close to smell which pack they belong to.

A loud howl runs through the compound, which has my hairs standing on end along my arms. The howl is quickly met by others as I hear people shouting as they wake up to chaos. A trio of wolves runs past me and I know it's the Alpha, Alex and Isa. I've seen Alex in wolf from before but I am still surprised by how big he is; he certainly rivals Mortlock in size. Alpha Mortlock has fur like my wolf, but while mine is more bronze, his is darker brown, mottled with black. He has a vicious snarl on his face as he dives towards some of the enemy wolves. Isa is large in her wolf form, but slimmer and leaner, her grey fur slightly longer than the male wolves. Alex barks at me as they race past, and I'm sure it's an order to shift.

I feel a pang in my chest and I know Killian is looking for me. My heart is torn. I want to go with Alex but I need to know that Killian and Seb are safe. Not to mention Gloria and my patients. I try to calm my mind, my wolf going into overdrive wanting to protect those who are *ours*.

I decide to ignore that little thought for now. Since when did I become so possessive?

"Ari!" I hear called out and I spin, finding myself in Killian's arms, my face buried in his chest.

I take a deep breath, inhaling his scent. I only then realise that he is doing the same, his face nuzzled into my neck.

"It seems that the warning was true," Killian tells me as he pulls away enough to look at me.

I go to reply but a loud growl has us turning towards the woods. A large grey wolf that I recognise is stalking towards us, his muzzle pulled back into a snarl. I curse as I see the long scar running down the wolf's face.

"It's the same wolf who attacked me. Guess we know who is behind this attack now," I tell Killian, but I'm not sure he is listening, his attention on the wolf in front of us.

The grey wolf snaps his teeth in my direction and Killian growls loudly, his body shaking as he fights his wolf.

"I know this bastard," Killian grits out, his voice barely human, and I know he is close to losing control to his wolf. "Protect the others. I've got this."

Jumping forward, Killian changes midair into the beautiful white wolf within him. I can't help but admire him for a few seconds before a scream cuts through my daydreaming. As I run towards the sound, I can't help but think it's not a coincidence that the two wolves I just left both have similar scars across their faces.

I fight against my wolf. I need to stay in control in case anyone gets injured. I rush around the corner when I see Seb backed up in front of one of the cabins in wolf form. Fear and anger rush through me. I've not seen Seb in wolf form before but somehow I know it's him. His fur is an auburn colour and he is much smaller in stature than the other wolves. He has two large wolves snarling at him and a bite on his front foot. I step closer and finally lose control of my wolf when I hear screaming inside the cabin. Jessica. My wolf rushes to the surface and I don't hesitate to let her take over as we become one.

I barely notice the sting of the change, adrenaline pumping through me. My change is fast, quicker than ever before, but I don't have time to think about that now. My thoughts and my wolf's are the same, finally in sync: neither of us is fighting the other. Our need to protect is running fiercely through our veins.

Seb is still facing off with the two stronger wolves, refusing to back down. Pride runs through us, my wolf seeing Seb in a different light. I snarl as I stalk up behind the other wolves, causing them to turn their back on Seb, thinking me the bigger threat. I don't give them a chance to strike me, darting forward and latching onto the bigger one's neck. I catch him by surprise and, as I bite down and twist my head, I hear a sickening crack of the bones in his neck breaking. A life taken so quickly, but I don't have time to think about that. I turn to fight the other one but Seb is already attacking him. He may be smaller and not have as much power, but he has been training for years and currently has the upper hand in this fight.

Another scream from inside the cabin has me running towards the sound; I know that Seb has this. Jessica needs my help. I run up the stairs and through the broken doorway, freezing at the sight before me.

"Ari!" a small, frightened voice calls out to me.

Jessica, Lottie and the other pack children are cowering in one corner, huddled together, with Gloria pinned to the ground by a wolf double her size.

"Ah, little wolf, you've finally arrived," Alpha Black says as he pushes away from the cabin wall where he had been leaning. I struggle to calm my breathing. I need to change back to human form. I need to be able to talk. I take a deep breath through my muzzle and pull my wolf towards my centre. The change back to human is easier than it has ever been. Perhaps my wolf can sense my urgency.

I stand, seeing that someone has left a long coat by the doorway. Bloody considerate of the bastard to leave me clothes out. I am surprised. I thought he would love me being vulnerable standing naked in front of him. I pull the coat on and scan the room, trying not to grimace at the fact that the coat smells like *them*. I realise now why they left the clothing. They are trying to prove ownership of me. I want to throw off the coat but I have more pressing matters. I glance around the room again. The children seem frightened but unharmed. Gloria is still, but breathing. I think she is unconscious until I see her eyes flutter.

"Gloria. Are you okay?" I call, not moving from my defensive position.

"Hello Ari, dear, I'm fine. Keep the children safe for me," she calls out to me. Even in a life-or-death situation, she is still caring for others, but I can hear the fear in her voice.

There are four members of Shadow Pack in the room: two grunts I don't recognise, Alpha Black and lurking in the corner of the room is Terrance, my childhood tormentor. I realise that someone else is here as he walks into my field of vision. I don't know how I missed him. Grinning at me like he has won the lottery is Marcus.

"You fucking traitorous piece of shit. You would betray your pack like that? Attacking those who are your kin?" I ask incredulously.

"They stopped being my kin when they sided with you, you bitch," he snarls, losing his composure. Terrance places a hand on his chest in warning.

The Alpha clears his throat, pulling my attention back to him. I bare my teeth at him in a snarl, anger filling me.

"Why the fuck are you here? What do you want?" I demand, my anger fuelling my words.

Alpha Black's knowing smile drops into a frown as though he is disappointed in my question.

"Oh, Ariana, you know better than that. We are here to take you home," he tells me, ending his statement with a smile, like we are a having a happy family reunion.

That sounds like him. He has come to get me, but he has to cause as much pain and suffering in the process. I think that this is a little dramatic for the likes of Alpha Black. Usually he goes straight for the jugular, unless there is something in it for him.

"That place was never a home, and if you think I'm going back with you, you're deluded. Especially after you have hurt my friends."

"That is no way to speak to your father," the Alpha comments lightly, and I shake my head angrily, spitting at his feet.

"You lost all privilege of me calling you that the day you tortured me to access my powers," I fume, mourning for the childhood I never had.

His expression turns into a frown. His eyes flick over my shoulder and I'm made aware of someone standing in the doorway behind me. Killian. The Alpha turns to look at Terrance before turning back to me.

"Aren't you going to greet your mate?" he goads, trying to make me slip up and make a mistake.

Killian growls and goes to step forward, but I block his path with my arm.

"*I* am her mate," Killian growls, but he doesn't make a move towards the others, instead trusting my judgement and standing at my side.

Alpha Black raises his eyebrows in surprise. Terrance has pushed away from the wall and looks like he wants to tear into Killian.

"My, my, you have been busy. Our little wolf is full of surprises," the Alpha muses, his tone even so that I can't tell what he is thinking. "I will cut you a deal, Ariana. Come with us and I will call off the attack."

It sounds like a genuine offer, but I know that nothing is ever that simple with Shadow Pack. I would rather die than go back, but I'm also not prepared for my new family to get hurt any further because of me.

"Don't even think about it," Killian growls in my ear. I turn my head toward him slightly, my eyes staying on the Alpha and Terrance.

"Killian–" I begin before he cuts me off.

"That self-sacrifice bullshit is exactly the type of thing you would do. Remember, I can feel your intentions. Besides, I don't trust this bastard to honour his word."

I nod. He's right. Damn it.

There are suddenly lots of loud noises outside of the house. Killian spins and snarls at something behind him. He races out the door, bursting into his wolf form midair.

"That's our cue to go," Alpha Black states.

Terrance stalks towards Gloria and kneels down next to her. Meeting my gaze, he has a sick smile on his face that I recognise all too well. I start moving before I have even realised. My shadow powers are pushing at me to let them out, but I fight against it. I don't know if I can control it and I don't want to hurt the children. But this is a mistake that will haunt me – I am too slow.

Partially shifting his hand, his claws slice through her neck. Everything goes in slow motion. I see her look at me before her eyes widen as she gasps for air.

I wordlessly scream and run at Terrance, pummelling my fists into him, not aiming for anywhere in particular, just trying to cause as much damage as possible. I am so focused on Terrance that I don't hear someone come up behind me. Something sharp stabs me in the shoulder but I ignore it, until my vision goes blurry and my arms go weak. I fall to the ground, my body going numb. The last thing I see before my vision goes are Gloria's wide eyes, her hand stretched out towards me. Blackness encompasses me and I can feel myself being lifted. A mournful howl is the last thing I hear before unconsciousness claims me.

Chapter Twenty Two

"Why didn't you save me?" Gloria asks, her neck wound gaping as she looks up at me from the ground. Betrayal and disappointment are clear in her eyes.

"You let me down. Now Jessica has to grow up without a mother, because of your incompetence," she continues.

I shake my head in denial, even though every word she says is true. I did let her down. I should have acted sooner. Poor Jessica is never going to speak to her mother again, and Seb... My heart clenches. How can I ever look him in the eyes again?

"Seb is going to hate you for letting me die," she says, as if she can read my mind.

"Gloria, I am so sorry. I will take care of them for you. I'm so sorry," I repeat, my heart breaking at the glazed look in her eyes.

Chemicals burn my nose, irritating my sensitive sense of smell. My brain is foggy and I am struggling to make sense of where I am. Flashes of Gloria's distraught and disappointed face float through my mind as I try to comprehend what is going on. I jerk upright as a stab of panic runs through me. Gloria.

My vision swims and I throw my arms out to steady myself, my hands connecting with cold concrete walls. My breathing picks up as I try to focus, the dream playing through my thoughts. I hiss in frustration as my memories evade me, and look around the room to try and make sense of things. *Think, Ari. Focus on what you* do *know as opposed to what you don't.*

At this point it seems obvious that I was drugged, given the foggy state of my brain and the unknown location I am currently in. I look around the room, taking stock of all the details. I am alone in a small, undecorated room, a single bulb hanging from a light fitting above me, the dim lighting not quite permeating the corners of the room. I am on the floor with a plain blanket thrown over me. It's cold in here, and I get the feeling that we are underground. My wolf agrees with my assessment; we are far from the moon. I am not on Moon River property and I can't pick up any smells over the reek of cleaning chemicals, which have no doubt been used to wipe any trace of who was previously here. This tells me that whoever brought me here went through a lot of trouble to hide their tracks.

I try to keep my thoughts clear but the dream keeps creeping back in, and I can't shake a deep sadness that is running through me. I try to run through the last thing I can remember. I was woken up in the middle of the night... screams... the sound of feet running... paws... Killian... Seb. An attack on Moon River Pack. Everything comes back to me in a flash and a blinding grief hits me and threatens to overwhelm me. Gloria is dead. Shadow Pack killed her.

I don't know how to deal with this vast feeling of loss and grief, especially as I am in unknown territory – I assume at the hands of Shadow Pack given the circumstances of my capture. I do the only thing I know how to do: I channel the dark anger that lurks at the centre of my being and I let it overcome me until my thoughts are quiet, focusing purely on my hatred for Shadow Pack. Seb's face flashes in my head and I use it to fuel my anger. I can't think about how distraught he will be over the death of his mother, or the fact I couldn't stop it, as it might threaten to break me.

I push up from the cold ground with shaky limbs and pace the sparse room I have been placed in. The metal door looks solid; it would need to be to hold a shifter in. I run my hands across it and test the handle: locked. No surprise there. I run my hands along the walls and count my steps from one side of the room to the other. I need to know everything about this room if I stand a chance of escaping. Unfortunately, I have been kept in rooms like this before so I know the drill. A flashback threatens to overcome me, but I force it back with the cold rage that has taken over.

I'm not sure how long I have been here. Time passes strangely in captivity. The sound of footsteps alerts me to someone coming my way and the sense of déjà-vu makes me want to laugh. They have done this on purpose, most likely to 'teach' me my place. I lean against the wall in the far corner, crossing my arms as a key turns in the lock. A familiar figure fills the doorway and I smirk in a way I know will piss him off.

"Hello, Terrance. Fancy seeing you here."

Terrance throws me a look of disdain at my smirk and greeting, probably disappointed that I'm not cowering in the corner. Sorry, mate, you picked the wrong girl. I smile, a sick part of me pleased that I have on some level messed up his little fantasy of getting me back. A cold glint enters his eyes as he smiles back at me, but it's not a friendly smile. It's the evil kind of smile you would expect from a psychopath.

"Lets see if you're still smiling after what we have planned for you," he tells me as his eyes run over me.

I just raise my eyebrow at his comment; other than that, I don't move a muscle. I know they killed Gloria to try and weaken me, but what they don't realise is that they have pushed aside my soft human feelings. Only anger reigns here now. If he is disappointed at my lack of reaction, he doesn't show it as he gestures forward, four unknown lackeys filling the hallway behind him. Even if I weren't still feeling the effect of the drugs, I would have struggled to fight against four shifters of this size, and whatever they used on me is silencing my connection with my wolf and my shadow powers feel far away. They corner me in the small room and I snarl at them as they reach for me. I punch at the guy closest to me and manage to throw the next guy that grabs my shoulder. Turns out my repetitive training with Killian did some good, after all. However, eventually they overpower me and drag me from the room, Terrance following behind with a sick smirk on his face.

Pain racks my body as I shift positions on the hard floor, but I refuse to let out the moan that moving elicits. I am not sure how long I have been here, but I have endured five 'questioning' sessions so far, which is their bullshit name for torturing me for information.

All of the sessions go the same. They drag me into another room, where they beat me until Terrance is happy. He then takes over, asking me all about Moon River Pack, trying to work out my connection with them, who my friends are, who I care for. And his biggest question: whether I have mated with anyone. He wants to know if Killian's claim is true. My scent has changed and it's driving him crazy, but I don't smell like Killian. If we had truly mated, he would have been able to sense the bond. Once they realise physical beating isn't going to make me talk, they move onto psychologically hurting me. Talking of how he killed Gloria, how weak she was and that she deserved to die. How her kids would be motherless because I wasn't strong enough to save her. This is nothing that I don't already know, but it is starting to get to me.

I try to keep my wall of anger strong, but the pain and lack of food is making it hard for me to keep my resolve. The fact that they keep me drugged is also not helping. It is smothering my senses and I keep thinking I can hear Killian's voice in my head. I know it's a hallucination, as he is being nice to me, telling me it's not my fault and to stay strong. I keep getting this annoying pulling sensation deep in my chest every time I feel like giving up and just giving into the pain. It feels like a kick in the chest. Had I not been so drugged up, I might have paid more attention to it, but right now I just put it down to being in so much pain that I am feeling things that aren't real.

The sound of footsteps alerts me to my daily wake-up call. I push up from my curled-up position on the floor and lean against the wall, not strong enough to stand. The door opens and I smile up at my tormentor.

"Hey Terry! Ready for my daily dose of torture?" I mock him.

Something I've learnt is that he hates it when I talk to him like this. It drives him mad that I'm not treating him with the respect that he feels he deserves from me. It makes the beating worse, but an angry, out of control Terrance is better than the sick, calculating Terrance that I know all too well.

"Bring her," he tells the guys behind him, ignoring my comment. But I can tell it got to him by the tick in his expression.

I smirk and try to push down the feeling of dread that is rising up in me as they drag me to the room I have affection-ately started calling the torture chamber. I refuse to admit it, but the moments when I am alone in my cell I have begun to feel numb, the pain filling my every thought, and as much as I try to push it away, grief and remorse have started to press against my wall of anger. So as much as I hate Terrance and his abuse, it helps to fuel my anger, even if just while I am in this room.

I am dumped unceremoniously onto the same chair in the middle of the room. The room is a little bigger than the cell that I am kept in, but it is brightly lit and painted all white. It must be a bugger to keep clean seeing as I keep bleeding all over it, and the sharp smell of cleaning chemi-cals tells me that I am right. The biggest difference between this room is that one wall is filled with a mirror that I am pretty sure is a one-way mirror. I wave at the mirror, before grimacing at my appearance: not pretty. I haven't seen the Alpha since I was brought here, but I'm pretty sure he has been watching from behind the mirror.

Someone is controlling Terrance and stopping him from going too far.

"Morning, Terry, what's the plan for today?" I quip at him, enjoying the snarl that lets me know my comment has reached its mark. He really is easy to annoy.

He looks over his shoulder and nods towards the mirror before addressing the lackeys filling the space in the room.

"You can go," he orders them. They glance at each other before nodding and leaving the room.

Hmm. That's different. Different makes me nervous.

"Today is going to go a little differently," he tells me, echoing my thoughts as he paces up and down the room.

"Tell me about Moon River Pack," he orders. The question is the same as usual and I ignore him.

I look back into the mirror and shake my head at my bruised face. My hair hangs dirty and unwashed and even in my drugged-up state I almost don't recognise myself. I look down at my nails and tut at the broken, dirty state I find them in.

"I need a manicure," I mutter to myself.

The hit to my face takes me by surprise as I was looking down. Ooh, the punishments are starting early today. Lucky me. I look up at Terrance's face as he looms over me.

"I said things are going to be different today," he spits, as his anger takes over him. I can see as he tries to push it away and straightens up, a worrying gleam entering his eyes.

"There is no point in fighting it any more, Ariana. Alpha Black has given me permission to mate you. You are mine now. You just need to agree to the bond."

I snort and roll my eyes.

"You really know how to proposition a girl, Terrance. You didn't seem to understand when I said no before, but I will say it again. Hell. No," I calmly tell him.

Internally I am filled with dread, but I am pleased that my voice doesn't betray that fact.

He has the audacity to laugh at me as he starts to pace the room again, his gaze running over me. The look in his eyes makes me feel sick and I have to fight to hide the shudder that runs through me.

"You think you have a choice in this?" He laughs again, turning and stalking towards me. "I know you have people you care about in Moon River. I will train that out of you. You belong to me now. If you agree to play along and behave, then I promise not to go back and slaughter the rest of the pack."

I feel like I have lead in my stomach and have to fight against the urge to vomit. Visions of Shadow Pack slaughtering my friends and the pack fill my mind with fear. I can tell when he senses my internal panic, as his smirk gets wider.

"I will never submit to you," I spit at him, watching as his smirk changes to a snarl. I will never trust his promise not to hurt them. He would probably hunt them out of spite.

"You think this is bad? Things can get so much worse for you."

He hits me again and the force has me falling to the floor. He pins me in place and I fight under him and he forces my shoulders down onto the ground.

"That boy you care for, the one whose mother I killed? He will watch as I mate you and we seal the bond with our bodies. And that bear that you slept with? Oh yes, I know all about him. I can smell him on you. He will be the first to die, but not before I make him watch the bonding too," Terrance torments me, his voice thick with desire as he talks about fucking me in front of my friends before killing them.

"You really are one twisted bastard," I spit. His words have refuelled my anger as I struggle under him, causing him to refocus on keeping me in place.

He ignores me and his hand reaches for his belt, filling me with horror.

"Let's get some practice in, shall we?" he asks, as he removes his belt, releasing my shoulders as he straddles me and works at his clothing.

This is a totally different type of torture that I was not prepared for and it threatens to crack my wall of anger. He is about to hurt me in the most intimate way and panic claws its way through my body.

"Fight it, Ari! Snap the fuck out of it and fight him!" hallucination-Killian orders me.

He may just be a figment of my imagination, but he is right. I won't just let Terrance take that piece of me without a fight.

I start thrashing with renewed vigour, clawing at his arms and biting any piece of him that comes too close to my face. Swearing, Terrance has to stop undressing to pin me down once more. Shouting out a name I don't recognise, he struggles with holding me down until I hear the door open and one of the lackeys from before lumbers in.

"Hold her down," he orders with a snarl.

The guy does as he is told, forcing my shoulders into the ground as Terrance reaches forward, ripping my top open, causing buttons to fly across the room. Even the evil lackey looks disturbed.

"Um, Sir? Alpha Black said not to–" he begins before he is cut off.

"Shut the fuck up and hold her down!" Terrance practically screams, the lackey paling and nodding at the orders from his Beta.

"Terrance, don't cross this line," I tell him, pleased that my voice doesn't show the terror that is running through me.

His hand gropes at my breast as I struggle against the hold of these men. Terrance leans over me, pressing his face against the side of mine so I can hear his rapid breathing in my ear. His erection is pressed against my stomach and he grinds against my body.

"I will make you forget about them. Eventually you will only think of me. I will kill anyone who dared to touch you," he whispers into my ear, his breath hot against my skin.

Anger takes over my body, filling me with a deadly calm I have only experienced once before.

"Hold on, Ari, fuel that anger. We are nearly there," hallucination-Killian orders me.

I do exactly as he tells me, my body stilling. I feel Terrance relax his weight over me, thinking I have given in to his sick groping of my body.

"Didn't your mother ever tell you that no means no?" I whisper back into his ear, before rearing up and smacking my head into his.

Leaping off me, Terrance clutches at his head as blood streams from his now-broken nose. I ignore the pain that I inflicted on myself, focusing on the anger running through me. Remembering Killian's training, I twist my body, trying to get out of the lackey's hold on my shoulders, using his shock and weight against him. With him now on the floor, I straddle him and brace my weight against his shoulders before he realises what is going on. With the cold rage fuelling me, I place my hands on his neck and twist, hearing the sickening snap of his neck. His eyes go wide before his body goes limp under me.

I push myself up on shaking legs before turning to look at Terrance. He is staring at me in shock, his hands still on his profusely bleeding nose. I take a step towards him before I hear shouting in the distance. Terrance swears and spins on his heel, sprinting out of the room and down the corridor. I swear and try to follow him before reality hits me at what just happened. I was nearly raped and I just killed a guy. I try to focus on my anger again, but reality is taking over. I stumble out of the room towards the sounds of fighting before pausing at the end of the corridor. I have no guarantee that whoever is fighting Shadow Pack is any more on my side than Terrance was. Thankfully, I am saved from making that decision as a furious Killian rounds the corner.

"Ari!" he shouts, his voice cracking as he runs towards me.

He goes to touch me and I flinch away from the sudden contact. He stops in his tracks as he registers my ripped shirt and my reaction to being touched. I can see him vibrating in fury as he comes to conclusions about what happened to me.

"Killian, now is not the time. We need to get her out of here." Seb's voice fills the corridor and I look around to see my friend.

I have never been so glad to see my guys – well, two of them anyway. Seb looks at me like he wants to embrace me but I can tell he is trying to give me space. Besides, Killian would probably blow a gasket if he touched me right now. I am surprised at how he is talking to Killian, though, and even more surprised when the stronger shifter nods stiffly in agreement.

"Can you walk?" Killian asks me softly.

I nod, wanting nothing more than to surround myself with my guys, but not now. Not here, while I still have the feel of Terrance's hands on my body. They lead me down a series of twisting corridors until we come to a larger room, which is full of bodies. Alex is in the centre of the room, panting as he breaks one of the lackey's necks, dropping the body to the ground. He looks up as we enter the room and an emotion I don't recognise fills his face.

"Ari," is all he says before he notices how I am cradling my body. His face hardens before he and Killian nod at each other. I don't know what they are communicating to each other but I just want to get out of here. I can hear fighting in other rooms so I assume other members of the pack are here, which means that Moon River Pack is at risk.

"Please, can we just go home to the pack?" I ask and I see their faces soften.

"Killian, Seb, can you take her back? I'll finish up here," Alex tells them.

They both nod and Seb offers me his hand. Killian looks like he is about to protest but when he looks at me his expression softens, as if he can see that I need this small act of comfort right now. I take Seb's hand and they silently lead me out of the building. I numbly walk over to one of their cars and climb in, dimly wondering when the pack had become home.

Chapter Twenty-Three

I scrub at my skin, trying to get the feeling of Terrance's hands off my body. The water of the shower is nearly scalding and it does nothing to help the pain of my bruised and cut body, but this is something I need to do to feel sane. Tori is waiting on the other side of the bathroom door for me while I shower. When we got back to the compound and the boys walked me to my room, I burst into tears when I saw her sitting on my bed. She had gently wrapped her arms around me and shooed the guys away. Killian had protested but didn't dare piss off a witch.

My skin is raw and red from standing under hot water for such a long time and, with a sigh, I turn off the shower. The room falls silent and I numbly pat myself dry, trying to avoid the worst of the bruising. A soft knock come from the door and I pull on an old pair of Seb's PJ bottoms and a soft t-shirt of Killian's that they had left for me to change into. They knew I had clothing here, but all of it was too tight and fitted to wear comfortably while I am still so bruised. I inhale the scent of the guys and it makes me feel stronger. The knock comes again.

"Ari. Are you okay in there? The guys want to see you." Tori's soft voice reaches me.

I look at myself in the mirror and shake my head. I look

broken. When did I become this person? I open the door and smile at Tori, my gut clenching at her soft smile.

"Let's go face the music," I tell her before striding out of the room – well, as well as someone as hurt as me can stride.

Once I reach the bottom of that stairs – with lots of swearing, mind you – I come to a stop as I see everyone gathered in the medical office. My office. I walk slowly into the room and take stock of who is here. Alpha Mortlock and Lena are here, along with Alex and Isa. Killian looks pissed off in the corner, but my eyes are drawn to Seb, who looks different. He is radiating more power than I have ever felt from him, not as strong as the others in the room but enough to make me stop in my tracks. He is smiling at me but I can see that he is grieving deeply for the loss of his mother. Guilt hits me and I wonder what the result of this meeting will be. The attack was my fault, after all. If I wasn't here, then Shadow Pack would have left them alone and Gloria wouldn't have been killed.

"She is blaming herself for the attack," Killian growls from the corner.

Everyone's eyes flick to him, then back to me, varying looks of shock and anger on their faces. How on earth does he know that? I thought my poker face was pretty good. I can feel the anger and frustration rolling off him towards me, and a part of me wants to go over and comfort him. I push that away. Now is not the time.

"Ari–" Alpha Mortlock begins, before Alex strides forward, a look of anger on his face.

"Why the fuck would it be your fault? Don't let those sick fucks make you think that any piece of this is your fault," he practically shouts at me.

I raise my eyebrows at his outburst, rarely seeing this much emotion or anger from Alex. What is winding him up so much that he would lose his usual professional cool? I have seen him playful and flirty, but never this angry.

"If anything, it is my fault," he says. "I am protector of this pack. As Beta, it is my job to anticipate threats like this. You even warned us and I still let it happen! Because of my failings, they killed Gloria and the others. They took you and I couldn't find you!" he continues, his voice breaking as he finishes.

Ah. That's why he seems so angry. He is blaming himself. A feeling of belonging and a warm emotion I don't have words for fill me at his words. Alpha Mortlock places a hand on Alex's shoulder in comfort, but Alex's eyes are glued to mine.

"I thought we had lost you. They had hidden all traces of where they had gone or where you were," he continues brokenly.

"He is right, Ari, you are not to blame. Nor are you, Alex. This was the sick minds of the Shadow Pack," Alpha Mortlock tells us, and I can hear the truth in his words. He fully believes what he is saying. He doesn't blame me. A weight I didn't realise I had been carrying lifts from me and breathing feels a little easier.

"There was magic involved in getting Shadow Pack out of the compound." I spin around at Tori's voice.

I still wonder at how she is here; I haven't had the chance to ask her yet. She walks further into the room and puts her arm around me as she leans against the counter, giving me comfort with her touch.

"When you disappeared, Alex called me to see if I could help." I glance over at Alex in surprise, knowing his feelings around witches. He was civil with Tori when she visited but I knew he was uncomfortable around them. He must have been desperate to find me to contact Tori. "I went to the place you were taken and tried a tracking spell. I used everything I know and I couldn't find you. You know me, Ari; tracking spells are my thing!" she states earnestly, and I can tell from her voice that she is feeling guilty that she couldn't track me.

"I eventually did a spell that proved that magic had been used, but I couldn't break through it – which means that a strong witch or warlock is involved," she concludes and, glancing round the room, I can see the others nodding in agreement.

"What we now need to work out is why would a witch or warlock help Shadow Pack? And where have they gone now?" Alpha Mortlock asks, looking to me for inspiration.

"As far as I know, they never had any contact with any magic users while I was held captive with the pack." I see my guys flinch at the mention of my abduction. "But I wasn't exactly privy to that kind of information," I state, running my hand though my still-damp hair in frustration.

I bite down on my lip and look up to meet Alpha Mortlock's eyes, dreading this question. "Did we lose anyone else? What happened?" Out of the corner of my eye, I see Seb flinch at the unmentioned fact that his mother had been killed.

The Alpha sighs and nods, pulling Lena closer into his side, her arm wrapping around him. Her eyes are red and puffy, like she has been crying.

"We lost a couple of our wolves during the attack, along with Gloria. We also lost a wolf when we managed to track you down. Although their deaths are a tragedy, it could have been much worse. Thanks to your warning, we were more prepared," he tells me, his voice soft as he talks of the dead.

"We killed all of the shifters in the building you were in, except for the Beta – Terrance, is it?" Growls filled the room at his name, surprisingly not just coming from me. The loudest one comes from Seb, who looks like his wolf is going to burst out of his skin.

Alpha Mortlock nods in agreement at the frustration in the room and keeps a wary eye on Seb as he continues.

"Unfortunately, he escaped. We are not sure how. We suspect magic was involved. We also couldn't find the Alpha."

I curse at his words. They won't give up trying to get hold of me. The best thing I can do is to leave so these guys don't get hurt any more. I know they don't blame me for what happened, but that doesn't stop the fact that as long as I am here, Shadow Pack will keep attacking.

"No." Killian's deep voice reaches me as he slowly walks towards me. I can see his body is tense, and as he approaches me, he keeps his movements slow, like he is worried he might startle me.

He places a hand on my waist and looks deeply into my eyes. I should feel crowded and want my space, but it feels right, him comforting me.

"You can't leave. You belong here, with us. Do you want to leave?" he asks, his tone demanding, like he needs to hear the answer.

I pause before I reply, admitting to myself what I have been trying to ignore for the last month: that I have felt more at home here with the pack than I have ever before, even living with Tori. The acceptance from the pack has made me care for them and I can't imagine not seeing them all again.

"No. I don't want to leave." My declaration rings around the silent room.

The sounds of relieved breaths fill the room and I see several smiles, including from Alpha Mortlock, who is being hugged by a beaming Lena.

"There is always a place for you here, Ariana," he tells me

warmly. I wince slightly at his continued use of my full name. Only Shadow Pack calls me Ariana; all my friends call me Ari. I will have to have a word with him about it, but now is not the time. I hate to break the somewhat happy mood but it's important.

"But how can I stay? Shadow Pack will keep coming for me. I can't put those I care about in danger over and over again," I admit, as I look around at those faces that have earned a place in my heart. I pause and frown. Someone is missing.

"Where is Garett?" I ask. I would have thought someone would have called him to tell him what had happened, even if they hadn't called him to help find me. I know the pack's relationship isn't the smoothest with him, but they accepted that he was important to me and should have informed him of something like this.

The mood in the room changes and the grim looks on their faces have me straightening, pulling away from Killian and Tori's touch.

"What are you not telling me?" I ask, my tone harsh with my worry.

"We tried to get in touch with him after you were taken and we couldn't find him. We contacted his pack and they haven't heard from him since yesterday. They are looking for him," Tori tells me, and I'm glad that it is her who breaks the news to me.

Worry fills me and I try to calm my thoughts; we don't know for sure that he has been taken. He is strong and would put up one hell of a fight. Sometimes Garett goes off the grid for a day or two – something about being one with nature. It's a bear thing.

"Okay, so what happens next?" I ask, clamping down on my fear for Garett. As soon as Tori and I are alone, I will get her to track him.

"Now we grieve our dead. Then we plan. Moon River does not just take an attack lying down. We demand justice." Mortlock's voice is firm as he says this and I can feel his Alpha strength fill the room. There is nodding around the room in consensus.

Everyone in the room breaks off into small groups, chatting quietly amongst themselves. People start to leave the room and Alpha Mortlock comes over and looks like he wants to place his hand on my arm but changes his mind.

"Are you okay?" he asks me, his eyes scanning over me, taking in my bruised appearance.

"No," I answer honestly. "But I will be," I tell him with a small smile.

"You know where I am if you need anything," he tells me with a small nod, before leaving the room.

Tori leaves the room with a small wave, gesturing that she is going back up to my room, leaving me alone with my guys. Well, all of them except Garett. My heart clenches at the thought of him missing. Killian notices and comes over to me, placing his hand on my cheek gently.

"He will be okay. And if he isn't, we will find him," he tells me seriously.

This is a different side of Killian that I have never seen before: softer, kind. I look into his eyes and can't stop myself as I lean forward and place a soft kiss against his lips. He freezes in shock before kissing me back, a slight groan leaving him as he presses against me.

The sound of feet moving towards me has me pulling away as I see Alex is standing next to us. He places his hand on my shoulder, rubbing it gently with his thumb.

"Killian is right. If anything has happened to him, we will

help you find him," he tells me, and from the sincerity in his tone I can tell that he means it.

I look between the two men giving me comfort and raise my eyebrows.

"We came to an agreement," Killian answers my unspoken question, his voice gruff as his eyes run over me again.

"What kind of agreement?" I ask warily, confused.

"When you were taken," Alex explains, "we realised that you were important to us and that we couldn't lose you. We then realised that you care for each of us, Garett included, and that any of us fighting over you is going to hurt you. We agreed that's not what we want and that we would no longer fight over who you care for."

I am gobsmacked and I look between the three of them before back to Killian.

"Wait, you agreed to this?" I ask, shocked that my Alpha wolf would fight against his instinct and the bond to agree to this.

He nods slowly, reluctantly as he looks from Alex to me.

"I don't like it, and it won't be easy. But I never want you to be hurt again, especially when it is my behaviour that is hurting you," he answers and I feel my eyes well up.

I look across at Seb. My funny, caring Seb. He is standing by himself on the other side of the room and I realise the guys had included him in the group of those I cared about. Seb and I hadn't explored that part of our relationship, trying to keep things strictly as friends even though our feelings may have wished otherwise. I walk over towards him, not sure of how I felt about all this, especially as Alex had apparently shared that he had feelings towards me.

"You agreed to this too?" I ask Seb softly, wincing slightly at the pain in his eyes.

"I'm not assuming anything. None of us are. If you don't

want a relationship with any of us, that's fine. We are not trying to push anything on you. But we also want you to know that we won't fight it. I don't know what might happen between us, but I know that I feel more for you than I ever have with anyone else, and I am sick of fighting it," Seb tells me, his voice stronger and more confident that I have ever heard it. "Mom wouldn't have wanted us to pussy-foot around our feelings," he adds, his voice heavy with grief.

"Seb," I start, my heart heavy. "I am so sorry about your mum." I break off, my voice tight and I see his eyes fill. "If you blame me for not being able to save her, I don't blame you. I feel the same," I tell him quietly, feeling as though my heart is breaking as he turns away from me.

His eyes shoot back up to me at my comment, his brows pulled into a frown. He turns so he is facing me again and walks towards me, backing me into my desk. Placing his hands either side of me, he has me trapped so I have nowhere to look but into his gorgeous eyes.

"You are not to blame. Never think that again. Do you hear me?" he demands, and I silently nod at my suddenly dominant Seb.

At my agreement he leans forward, placing his hand on my jaw and firmly pulling me towards him like he is going to kiss me. My emotions are a mess and I know there is a chance I might regret this later, but right now all I want is Seb's lips on mine, even though I know the other guys are watching.

"Ari!" Tori's panicked voice has me jerking away from Seb as she thunders down the stairs, my phone grasped in her hand.

The guys around me are instantly on alert and surround me as if to protect me. I push past them towards my best friend.

"What is it? What's wrong?" I demand as I hurry towards

her, my stomach dropping as I see the picture that has flashed up on the screen.

I turn away from her and lean against the wall for support as panic threatens to overwhelm me. Seb hurries to my side, placing a hand on my shoulder as Alex takes my phone from Tori, his face paling as he sees the graphic picture that has been sent to me, before passing it to Killian who snarls in response.

"They have Garett."

Chapter Twenty Four

The next few hours pass in a blur of arguing and planning, but finally we are on our way to find Garett. I wanted to go alone, as the message had stipulated, but was quickly shot down. Now, I am sitting in the back of my car with Seb and Killian, with Alex at the wheel.

"This is probably a trap," I mutter as I stare out of the car window.

They refused to let me drive, protesting that I was too injured. They all wanted me to stay behind, stating that I was what Shadow Pack wanted and they didn't want to risk them getting me. I had swiftly informed them that I would be going, and if they somehow left me behind I would just follow them. If they were looking for backup from Tori, they would have been disappointed, as she had just shrugged and told them I would find a way to get there anyway so they might as well take me. Isa and several of the pack defenders had wanted to come along. Even Alpha Mortlock had wanted to help, which had warmed my heart. Eventually it was agreed that the pack couldn't be left undefended in case this was a trap, especially so soon after the last attack. Besides, the Alpha is needed with his grieving and vulnerable wolves.

"That is exactly why we didn't let you go alone," Alex retorts as he drives towards the address sent to me.

The message contained the address where I was to meet them, stipulating that I was to go alone and that they wanted me in exchange for Garett. A second message had shown a graphic photograph of Garett, who had clearly been beaten. I try to control my breathing as the image flashes through my mind again, trying to contain my anger.

"They probably won't expect you to bring us. From what you have told us about Shadow Pack, they isolated you and made you distrust anyone. You've always been a lone wolf because of it, they are hoping that you'll run straight to them and sacrifice yourself for Garett without saying a word to us," Seb says from his seat next to me in the back of the car, his hand in mine.

Annoyingly what he is saying makes sense, as that is exactly what I was going to do. If I had seen the message before Tori, I would have snuck out on my own and done exactly that. Killian snorts from his seat and turns to look at me over his shoulder.

"We all know you are the self-sacrificing sort. Do you really think that we would let you go on your own?" he asks as I gape at him in offence.

"I am not the 'self-sacrificing' sort!" I retort, no idea what they are insinuating. "I run away from every situation that makes me uncomfortable," I continue, not sure why I am saying any of this out loud.

Alex looks at me through the rear-view mirror and gives me a slight smile.

"You only run away from commitment. If someone is in need, you would sacrifice yourself for them," he tells me firmly and I realise there is some merit in what he is saying.

"You accepted the challenge to defend me at the pack social and you ran into a fight, without thinking, to protect Jessica, even though you knew there would be dire consequences for you. Plus, you're a nurse. I would call that self-sacrificing," Seb chips in with a squeeze of my hand.

Huh, maybe they are right. I chew on my thumbnail as we get closer to the abandoned warehouse I have been directed to. I know, cliché right? The plan for us is to abandon the car a few miles out; the guys will shift into their wolves downwind and follow behind as I walk to the warehouse in my human form. They debated about this, but I argued that Shadow Pack will probably be watching out for me, and if they walk in with me they could do something to harm Garett. Seb was the one who suggested that they should follow behind in wolf form, to make sure I wasn't ambushed. I tried to convince him to stay behind. I'm worried that he is going to get hurt against such dominant wolves, but Alex spoke up for him and said he should come. He has been different since the attack: quieter, but more than that he *feels* different, stronger, more powerful.

I glance over at him, worry gnawing in my chest. He feels my gaze and turns to smile at me. It's a soft smile meant to comfort but I can see the grief in it, and there is a new hardness about him.

The car pulls to a stop and I take in a deep breath, calming my nerves and calling up the anger that had been boiling in me since the attack. I must now put on a mask. This is nothing new for me, but this time I must convince Shadow Pack that Garett is nothing more than a possession, taken without permission, that I am now here to reclaim.

The woods are silent save for the sound of my feet against the earthen ground. I can't see or hear the guys. They have done a good job of silently tracking me. If I didn't know they were following me, I wouldn't know they were there. The abandoned warehouse is in front of me and I look around for any signs of movement. This is an odd place for a warehouse. It must have been a privately owned building, as no company would store their merchandise out here in the middle of nowhere.

Keeping my steps strong and my shoulders back, I make sure I appear confident as I stride towards the old building. A feeling of foreboding hangs over me and I can't shake it. I know we are walking into a trap, and I can only hope that Seb is right and they will be expecting me to come alone. Chemicals burn at my nose and obscure my senses as I try to pick up their scents. I can hear shuffling and some low murmurs coming from inside the building, so I know that several people are inside.

As I step over the threshold, a tingling sensation runs across my body. Shit. I've just set off some sort of magical ward. If I was human I wouldn't be able to feel it but anyone with super-natural blood would be able to feel that. Dread lines my stomach and I turn to face the doorway I just walked through. Reaching out my hand, I curse as it hits an invisible barrier, confirming my suspicions. Once someone has crossed the ward, they cannot leave unless the one who controls it allows passage or dies. Meaning I am trapped. It also confirms that Shadow Pack have no intention of letting Garett go, even if I comply to their whims. I suspected as much but it is still a blow to my stomach.

"I can hear you, little wolf. Come in," Alpha Black calls.

Fighting against the urge to turn and run, I straighten my back and walk down the corridor into the main room of the warehouse. It's a large and mostly empty room, filled only with people and a single chair in the centre. There are about a dozen wolves in the room, one of which is the traitor Marcus. The Alpha and Terrance are standing by the chair and I meet their smirking faces, keeping my eyes away from the slumped figure on the chair. I want to run to Garett, fall to my knees and beg for his forgiveness. The nursing part of me is desperate to assess his injuries, worried about his breathing rate. However, I can't show any of that. Any sign of affection will be viewed as a weakness and I can't let them see how I care for him, as they will use that against me.

"Let's get this over with, shall we?" I state, looking over my enemies with a coldness in my eyes I rarely let show.

I see some of the wolves in the room flinch under my gaze, but if it affects the Alpha or Terrance they don't let it show. In fact, the Alpha's smirk grows, as if he knows that I am putting on a front.

"Are you ready to come home with us and take your rightful place among us?" Alpha Black asks. A knowing look has entered his eyes and it is making me nervous.

"I am here to reclaim what you have taken from me." I keep my voice firm and nod toward Garett.

I still keep my eyes off him, although the temptation to look, just to check he is okay, is almost overwhelming. Especially as at the sound of my voice he has been trying to lift his head, making pained noises and struggling against his bonds. I know he is trying to get to me, to protect me from these monsters that call themselves family. I know that I am going to have to say and do things in this room that will hurt him, but my main priority is keeping him safe and I hope he understands that.

"You expect me to believe that you have no feelings for this *bear?*" Alpha Black asks with a laugh and a shake of his head.

His tone of voice makes it clear what he thinks of me sleeping with a different race of shifter. Terrance has a similar disgusted expression on his face and is looking at Garett with hate in his eyes. It's not hard to guess that Terrance was the one to dole out Garett's beating. Another reason for me to kill the bastard. My wolf growls in agreement, eager to tear him apart for all he has put us through.

I feel a shudder run through me; magic brushes over my skin as my guys pass through the magical barrier. Part two of our plan has begun. Three snarling wolves dart into the room and start attacking the shifters in the room. They would have felt the ward on their way in, so they will know that we have to kill whoever controls the ward if we have any hope of leaving here alive. We may be outnumbered but we have surprise on our side.

The shock on Terrance's face is almost comical, and the Alpha looks impressed.

"I'm surprised at you, little wolf. You accepted help. Perhaps the lone wolf is ready to settle down, after all. I guess it's a good thing I installed the wards then," he smirks.

I shrug my shoulders. None of this is news to me. I had suspected he wouldn't just let us walk out. The magic had been a surprise, though.

"I knew this would be a trap. Not even you travel without

back-up, so why shouldn't I?" I ask with a shrug, trying to ignore the snarling and growling coming from the fighting wolves around me. Terrance has joined in the fight now. I don't like that he is out of sight, but I keep my eyes trained on the Alpha. "So, you have a mage doing your dirty work now?" I ask, keeping my voice even.

"I bought the wards off a mage. He didn't even know what they were for," he answers with a shrug.

This puts me at ease a little. Mages have the power to put certain spells into objects or paper, for example a ward spell like the one used here could be put onto paper to be activated in the desired place at a later date. The thought of Shadow Pack having direct access to a mage was a worry, so the fact he probably just bought this on the black market, while surprising, is not as disastrous. I am surprised that Shadow Pack is buying spells from mages, though. They are more racist towards other supernatural races than most shifters. I guess he takes a break from being a bigot when it suits him.

I start taking small steps towards the Alpha; we need to wrap this up quickly. I can see that Killian and Seb are covered in bite wounds and Alex is cornered by two smaller wolves, Marcus one of them, but the room is littered with bodies of the Shadow Pack. I am so focused on the Alpha that I fail to realise that Terrance is about to grab me until I'm too late. Caught in a bear hug, I try to struggle out of the hold using the technique that Killian taught me, but I can't shift my weight.

"Call off your wolves," Alpha Black demands.

He may have me trapped, but as I look around I see that we have the upper hand – we are winning. Killian has killed his opponent and is now helping Alex finish off the two who had him cornered.

I laugh, which turns into a grunt as Terrance squeezes me

harder threateningly, but I find that I don't care what they do to me. As long as my guys get out of here, Shadow Pack can do whatever they like. Huh, guess I am self-sacrificing after all.

"We will kill your *precious bear*," Terrance whispers cruelly into my ear.

My stomach twists but I know that was their plan anyway. I try to keep my face neutral, remembering the role I am playing. I attempt to shrug but it's difficult with my arms trapped by my sides.

"I don't trust you. Plus, I told you. I don't care. I just came to retrieve my property." The words burn my mouth as they come out.

I know I have made a grave mistake as the Alpha smiles at me. I know that smile. It's a cold, evil smile, like he is going to enjoy this moment.

"Then you won't care if he is dead or alive."

The world slows down and before he has even finished his sentence I am on the move. Calling down to the dark part of my soul, I call forward my Shadow self. I let go of the hard-earned control that usually keeps that part of me on lockdown and let her take full control. With all my inhibitions gone, my Shadow self acts faster than those in the room can blink.

My body ghosts out of existence, slipping from Terrance's hold, darting forward to the Alpha. We watch as his hand slowly moves towards Garett's exposed neck with a blade he must have had concealed somewhere. Gripping the knife, my body returns solid as I twist the knife from his grip, slicing across his neck. I watch numbly as my father's blood covers me and he falls limply to the floor.

"Ari..." Garett's broken voice breaks me out of my stupor.

I spin around and drop to my knees in front of him, placing my hands on his face, needing to feel him, to know he is okay. I press my forehead to his, relief spreading through me. Suddenly a sharp pain shoots in my head and a wave of dizziness nearly knocks me to the ground.

I've gone too deep – let go of too much control. There is a price to be paid with Shadowborn powers. I can feel the Shadow Dimension tugging at my soul. I don't know what will happen on the other side. Grief strikes through me at the thought of losing the guys just as I am beginning to acknowledge that there may be something worth fighting for.

"I love you, Ari," Garett whispers tiredly, I can hear the love in his voice even after everything that has happened.

My heart warms and I find that I don't mind sacrificing myself if it means that Garett and the guys are safe.

"I love you too," I whisper to him, my eyes filling with tears. I lean forward and press a kiss to his lips.

With a cry, I feel my soul being ripped from my body as I fade into the Shadow Dimension.

The last thing I see is my lifeless body with Seb and Killian running to surround me, and Garett, still restrained to the chair screaming my name.

Now all I know is darkness.

ACKNOWLEDGMENTS

Firstly I would like to thank my wonderful team of beta readers, I literally wouldn't be able to do this without you. Thank you to my lovely editor who makes my words actually make sense.

To my family who put up with me whilst I was writing this and acted as sounding boards for all my ideas.

And most importantly, thank you to all our amazing readers who have taken time to read this book. Blood, sweat and tears have gone into this, so I really appreciate all the comments and support.

ABOUT THE AUTHOR

Erin is originally from the UK, works full time within the Healthcare system and writes in her free time.
She is married and loves going on adventures with her husband and making him listen to her new book ideas. She has no children but one fur baby who keeps her on her feet.
She is a reading fanatic, loves video games and is addicted to coffee.

Come and join me on my readers page over on Facebook for updates, competitions and general silliness!

https://www.facebook.com/groups/2091459094400242/

Printed in Great Britain
by Amazon